THE SHUT-IN

JAMES PATTERSON is one of the best-known and biggest-selling writers of all time. His books have sold in excess of 325 million copies worldwide. He is the author of some of the most popular series of the past two decades – the Alex Cross, Women's Murder Club, Detective Michael Bennett and Private novels – and he has written many other number one bestsellers including romance novels and stand-alone thrillers.

James is passionate about encouraging children to read. Inspired by his own son who was a reluctant reader, he also writes a range of books for young readers including the Middle School, I Funny, Treasure Hunters, House of Robots, Confessions and Maximum Ride series. James has donated millions in grants to independent bookshops and he has been the most borrowed author in UK libraries for the past nine years in a row. He lives in Florida with his wife and son.

THE SHUT-IN

JAMES PATTERSON

WITH DUANE SWIERCZYNSKI

BOOKSHOTS

5 7 9 10 8 6

BookShots
20 Vauxhall Bridge Road
London SW1V 2SA

BookShots is part of the Penguin Random House group of companies whose addresses can be found at global.penguinrandomhouse.com.

First published by BookShots in 2017

www.penguin.co.uk

A CIP catalogue record for this book is available from the British Library.

ISBN 9781786530967

Printed and bound in Great Britain by Clays Ltd, St Ives Plc

THE
SHUT-IN

CHAPTER 1

COME, FLY WITH ME.

That's it—up, up and away. Don't be afraid. I've got you. Everything's going to be all right.

We float up one story…two stories…three stories…and there, we've just cleared the edge of the rooftops.

If you're nervous, don't look down. Just look *out*… at the skyline of Philadelphia, my adopted hometown. Falling away below us is my neighborhood, Spring Garden, just on the fringes of Center City.

Let's soar a little higher, shall we?

(Don't worry. I'm not going to drop you.)

It's just after eight, which means lots of people will be making their way downtown for work. Prime people-watching time.

An endless variety of people—millennials with their gelled hair and too-tight jeans, probably off to work at some start-up with exposed beams, reclaimed wood, and a foosball table. Lawyer-types in their fine suits and even more expensive shoes who will spend their days in air-conditioned conference rooms. Ordinary Philly dudes in jeans and button-down shirts, trying to make it to 6 p.m. as fast as they possibly can.

Or take a look at the middle-aged woman just below us. She's probably in her late forties or early fifties, wearing business attire that's at least a decade out of style. Maybe she moved to Spring Garden full of excitement twenty years ago and never quite figured out how to leave. She walks like her feet hurt. The last thing she wants to do is shuffle downtown to an office where she's ignored or undermined at every turn.

She stops at the corner of 19th and Brandywine, looking up at the bus route sign, then seems to think better of it. Instead, she continues down 19th.

Go, girl, I want to tell her. *Fight the good fight.*

But all too soon, our time is up. We must glide back home. Which is a sad proposition as much as it is a delicate one.

Because if we don't stick the landing in just the right way, we're going to end up splattered all over the side of this building.

CHAPTER 2

NO, YOU WEREN'T just floating along with a friendly neighborhood guardian angel. I'm not dead, and you're not a ghost.

Those glorious city views are courtesy of my personal drone, *Amelia*. I send her out every morning and evening to see a bit of the world that I can't.

I pilot *Amelia* using an app on my smartphone. The controls are super sensitive, so getting her to zoom back in through my rear window without knocking off a propeller takes a bit of finesse. When I first bought *Amelia,* she bumped into the side of my brownstone building so many times I'm surprised she's still in one piece.

Some lucky drone owners are able to go outside into an empty field and launch their quadcopters straight up into the air.

But not me.

My name is Tricia Celano. Call me "Trish" at your own peril. I'm twenty-five years old, live in a small but sweet studio apartment at 20th and Green, and if I step outside, the sun will kill me.

No, for real.

I have a condition called *solar urticaria,* which is a rare allergy to the sun. Yes, the same ball of swirling gas ninety-three million miles away that gives everything else the gift of life wants to give me a severe case of death.

My symptoms were minor back in college—hives, itching, burning. But soon I was breaking out in severe body rashes that made me look like a lobster–human mutant hybrid. By senior year, the condition was so severe that I stayed in my room to finish classes remotely and even had to sit out my graduation.

All of which turned me into a twenty-five-year-old shut-in—confined to my apartment all day, every day.

But you'd be surprised how easy it is to live your entire life indoors. Before the internet, I'm sure I would have withered away and died. But now I can order pretty much *everything* online—food, clothing, entertainment—and have it delivered, downloaded, or streamed straight into my apartment.

As for other forms of entertainment…well, sometimes I'll pull a Jimmy Stewart and spy on the people coming and going from my building. I especially like to watch the hot dark-haired guy who lives upstairs in 3-D. I've gotten to the point where I recognize the way he clomps down the stairs toward the entrance of the building just a few feet from my door. Usually it's a mad scramble to the peephole to catch even a tiny glimpse of him, and I don't think I've ever seen his entire face. But the parts that I have seen…

Anyway. You might say, *But Tricia, if you're allergic to the sun, why don't you just go out at night?*

Because…well, life really likes to stick it in and twist sometimes.

In the three years since graduation, I've also developed this oh-so-charming phobia of the dark. The very thought of stepping out into the night paralyzes me with raw, naked fear. Logically I know I'd be fine. But try telling my subconscious that.

Friends from college will try to coax me out for a drink, but…I just can't. Once I was even showered and dressed, make-up and hair done…and then broke down sobbing in the vestibule of my building.

I miss the outside world so very, very badly. Chatting through social media or even Skype doesn't quite fill the void. I yearn to be out in the world again, eating it, drinking it, bathing in it.

So, as I did with my other challenges, I came up with a technological solution.

Amelia—named after legendary aviatrix Amelia Earhart—is a ready-to-fly quadcopter with a built-in camera and absolutely no problems with the sun. She cost me a shade under three hundred bucks, but who can put a price tag on the feeling of being part of the world?

I can fly *Amelia* within a half-mile radius of my apartment, and her camera feed is sent straight to my cell phone in real time. She's my amazing, soaring window on the world. Or at least my tiny sliver of it.

Technically, I'm breaking the law. There's this thing in drone culture called "line of sight," or LOS, which basically means that you're supposed to keep visual contact with your drone at all times.

But the Philadelphia Police Department has bigger fish to fry than tracking a lonely girl's renegade drone. Which is a good thing. Because what started as a hobby has turned into a bit of an obsession. And now I'm not sure how I'd live without it.

I work as a marketing associate for an entertainment company with offices in California, Scotland, and Germany, so I find myself working at odd hours anyway. My day is broken up by *Amelia* flights, at least three per day. They span eleven minutes each, which is exactly how long her batteries last.

First flight is usually during the morning rush, when there's a lot of people to watch. Same goes for the evening commute. But lunchtime has become fun, too. I like to take *Amelia* downtown, just beyond the tightly packed rows of Victorian homes, where you can make out the Benjamin Franklin Parkway. It's modeled after the Champs-Élysées in Paris and is usually full of a mix of tourists and homeless people.

When darkness falls, however, it's game over. It's too risky to fly *Amelia* in the dark, and not just because of my phobia. The images on my phone are too dim to help me avoid the obstacles out there.

Night is when I feel most like a prisoner.

CHAPTER 3

BUT THIS IS a bright Thursday morning in early September, and it's time to send *Amelia* out into the world to see what's up.

Or down, as it were.

If you've ever used an app on your phone, you already know how to pilot a drone like *Amelia*. There's a little gray circle on the lower left that controls her altitude, and a bigger gray button on the right that controls her horizontal movements. If you hold the right button down, you can spin her around. Working all these buttons in tandem, however, is the tricky part.

I tap the green Fly button at the bottom of the screen, and we're up, up and away.

I send *Amelia* zipping down Green Street, then tweak the controls so she makes a smooth, gliding right onto 19th Street. Turns are the hardest thing to master. Play with the buttons too much, and *whammo,* you're kissing a brick wall.

When I want to play it safe, I take *Amelia* over the rooftops. But up there, it's too hard to see what all the people with real lives are doing. So I try to keep her no more than two stories above the sidewalk.

Amelia zooms down 19th Street, toward the Free Library.

Along this path there's a stunning amount of new construction—condos and restaurants, mostly. It's crazy how fast this stuff goes up. Sometimes I send *Amelia* out and I really have to study the images on my phone to figure out where the heck we are.

But instead of checking out the cranes and the construction guys—who don't catcall or wolf-whistle at a drone, by the way—I steer *Amelia* to one of my favorite places in the neighborhood: the old Philadelphia & Reading Viaduct that's currently under construction.

Most Philadelphians have no idea this thing is in progress. That's because its only access point is an unmarked opening on the block between Hamilton and Callowhill on 19th Street. But go past the caution signs…and it's basically a wonderland up there. And in the daytime, it's all mine.

I only happened upon it last month, and it took me a few weeks to work up the courage to fly *Amelia* directly above it. Even now, the very idea sends a flutter through my nervous system. Back in the late 1800s, it was a bustling railway that would carry steel to the Baldwin Locomotive factory. But then the twentieth century happened and it was no longer used. By the 1990s, the tracks were torn up for scrap. A few years ago, a group petitioned the Reading Railroad to turn the area into a public green space. In the meantime, however, they've sealed it off.

Too bad they can't seal it off from *Amelia*…

From above the abandoned space, I watch the sunlight cast its rays through the sidewalk grates. It's dim in the early morning light, but the space is brightened by the wild plant life that's already started to grow here. Some quick googling helped me identify the goldenrod, foxglove trees, and even a weird Southern magnolia that sprouted up in a lonely corner, as if in defiance of the northern climate. It's amazing.

Each time I visit, I push *Amelia* a bit further. I move her along the viaduct, hoping to catch a glimpse of something new.

Today does not disappoint.

Shockingly, there are two people here, right off the main chasm in clear violation of SEPTA rules. Now I'm sure urban spelunkers explore this place all the time, but I've never seen anyone here in the daylight hours. What could they be doing?

I pilot *Amelia* into a kind of hover mode up in the sky. I don't want to get too close and spook the people.

Keeping *Amelia* steady, I zoom in with her camera to take a better look. Are they punks, here to tag the construction signs along the viaduct? Or perhaps they're lovers who have snuck away for an early morning tryst?

Standing on the rock-strewn ground is a woman in business attire…and a few feet away, there's a man on his knees. If this is a tryst, it's clear who's boss in this relationship.

"Steady, girl," I tell *Amelia,* as if she can hear me. I zoom in closer, which pixelates the image a little. "I promise, if things get racy, I'll pull you out of there. Don't want you scandalized."

But things do not get racy.

Instead the man lifts his hands, as if he's pleading with the business woman. The woman walks toward him, lifting her left arm like she's pointing a remote control at a TV set.

Then something flies from her hand so quickly, it barely registers on the camera. But a second later, I see it clearly, because it is sticking out of the man's chest.

An arrow.

And the man keels over.

CHAPTER 4

Target Diary–Day 7

SUBJECT NUMBER FOUR falls down quickly.

But when I press my fingers to the side of his grimy, disgusting neck I find a weak but insistent pulse.

Disappointing.

Of my four in-field experiments thus far, only two have died immediately with a single shot—subjects Two and Three.

Death for Number One, like Four here, required a bit of extra effort.

I pull up my sleeve and load another arrow into my gauntlet. The wires bite into my fingertips as I pull them taut. I ignore the pain and enjoy the callusing effect. There's a sharp click.

I'm ready to go.

Number Four's eyes flutter open. At best, he's probably sixty seconds away from death. But you never know. Some human beings have been known to survive extreme body trauma for shockingly long periods of time. Number Four may be an indigent in poor health, but there's no accounting for his genetic stock. He may be one of those people who survive.

"Please," he's stammering now, his voice hushed. One of his

lungs has most likely collapsed. "You don't have to do this, I'm a nobody, lady, nobody..."

"Shhhh," I tell him.

"I thought you wanted to help me!"

I take careful aim, again, wondering how I'd miscalculated the first shot. The tip of the arrow is supposed to slip past the protective rib cage and strike the portion of the heart that will cause the organ to fail within seconds. I've done my homework. Had consultations with three different cardiovascular surgeons. Used a half-dozen cadavers from a black market medical supply concern for target practice early in the mission.

There is no substitute, however, for a live target.

"Please please please...."

Especially one who is squirming around like a maggot.

"Shhhh," I tell him, then take a few steps back. I want to perfect this shot at the proper distance. No sense cheating it now. The more practice I can log, the better my chances of success for the Big Day.

Now that he sees that I'm aiming, his writhing becomes even more erratic, as if he can somehow twist himself out of harm's way. This amuses me. A laugh bubbles up out of my throat, much to my own surprise. Number Four gawks at me, insulted, and stops twisting for a moment.

And that is exactly when I take my shot.

This time it's a perfect hit. A second after impact, the life visibly fades away from his rheumy eyes.

I take a moment in the silence to allow the last few seconds to imprint themselves onto my nervous system. So much of this profession is about the visualization and coordination of my muscles and brain.

Dilettantes waste those glorious moments after a successful hit. To me, they're everything.

But nevertheless, I am distracted. Because there's something out of place. A sound.

A buzzing sound.

CHAPTER 5

OKAY, NOW I'M freaking out.

Don't get me wrong, I was pretty much freaking out the moment I watched a business lady shoot *a freakin' arrow* into the chest of a poor homeless man.

But then, just as the guy was begging for his life and wriggling around like a worm on a fish hook...she shot him again! With another arrow!

And this time, it worked. He stopped wriggling.

Part of me is praying that what I've watched is some kind of elaborate form of street theater, a pretend assassination for the delight and amusement of commuters. Then I remember that no one can possibly see these two people, except if you happen to be flying a drone at a specific angle, high above the blocked-off viaduct.

This is no street theater. I've just witnessed a murder.

I'm frozen in place, my thumbs trembling as they hover above my phone screen. *Amelia* hovers, too—almost impatiently. *What are we going to do next, boss?*

"We're going to retreat, Amelia."

I pilot her straight up into the air, not wanting to bang her on the railings of the viaduct. But at the same moment, the business lady turns around, and for a fleeting moment, it's as if we've locked eyes.

Oh no.

She saw me.

Go go go go go, Amelia!

My thumbs do a desperate dance and poor *Amelia* is spinning and the image on the screen is chaotic and confusing.

Don't flake out now, Tricia, says a voice in my head. *Not when it counts.*

Because even in my panic, I'm formulating a plan. And the plan is this: take *Amelia* to a safe height, and then wait for this business lady and her arrows to emerge from the viaduct. There are very few ways in and out. Once I have a fix on her at street level, I call the police, and they can go scoop her up. As long as she stays in the quarter-mile range, I can follow her and lead the cops directly to her.

Miraculously, I'm able to stabilize *Amelia*. She's hovering above 20th Street, just up the block from those safe and familiar bastions of urban life—the hipster coffee shop, the organic grocery store. You know, civilized places, where people don't go around *shooting other people with arrows.*

But when I hold down the right button and spin *Amelia* around, I see a large white object coming right at us at approximately sixty-five miles per hour...

...and it's the top of a white delivery truck.

My thumbs go ballistic as I struggle to put as much distance between *Amelia* and the speeding truck as possible.

And I would have been successful, had it not been for this pesky building nearby.

Amelia crashes on the edge of the roof, right smack into an old metal frame that used to hold an ancient sign.

"No no no," I murmur as I futz with the controls. "Please don't be stuck..."

Good luck with that.

And the voice inside my head is right; it's no use. In my haste to escape, I somehow impaled poor *Amelia* on that old, rusty sign. She's pinned like a butterfly in a collection.

"I'm so sorry, honey," I say as I give up and power her down.

I'll have to mourn her later, though. I close out the app, then push 911 on my cell. This is the first time I've ever done such a thing in my life.

It's also the first time I've ever said the words:

"Hello? Um, I think I've just witnessed a murder..."

CHAPTER 6

Target Diary–Day 7 (continued)

I TURN TO look, but the sun temporarily blinds me. After shielding my eyes I'm able to make out a blurry shape rising out of view. The buzzing sound fades away.

It's entirely possible the two are unrelated. The buzzing may have been an echo of nearby traffic. The humming of a motorbike, for instance.

But I don't think so. My senses are finely tuned to notice any sights or noises that don't fit the usual patterns. This is also something a dilettante will ignore. But if something is coming for you, the environment will give you plenty of warning.

From my perspective, however, all seems normal.

I slip on a pair of latex gloves and prepare for the grunt work.

There's a fairly deep pit approximately a hundred yards from my current location. It is the current resting place of Numbers One through Three.

I grab Number Four by his wrists and begin to drag him toward it. I would usually pull the legs, but he's not wearing any shoes and the stench is already disgusting enough.

Yet, the disadvantaged are perfect for my needs, and abundant here in Philadelphia, especially near the Parkway. Many of them are wary, but it's easy enough to find the few who are willing to believe a perfect stranger is offering a hand up.

Some are even willing to believe that there might be more than a warm meal on offer.

Perhaps even a real personal connection, and a way out of a desperate situation.

I can spot the tiny flicker of hope in their eyes, and I'm just the person to fan it into a proper flame.

It helps, too, that my appearance is homely. This works to my advantage, because nobody trusts a gorgeous face.

Finally, I reach the edge of the pit. I can smell the others, decaying there. I crouch down and roll Number Four into the darkness with the rest of his kind. Thank you for your services.

Still, when I ascend back to street level, the mysterious buzzing sound that I heard continues to vex me. I walk around the neighborhood, searching for its possible source. I'd like to be able to put this out of my mind.

I head down Hamilton Street and watch the construction crews assemble yet another condominium. I stroll toward the Parkway, where tourists blindly flock to the museums, pay their entrance fees, and look at objects they are told are beautiful.

But they have no real appreciation for beauty. They possess neither the mental capacity nor the imagination for it.

The bodies in the pit. They are beautiful.

Nobody pays me any particular mind as I wander around. My garments are that of any workaday Philadelphian, on her way downtown for a pointless office job.

Which, frankly, is the whole point.

CHAPTER 7

THE KNOCKING IS so loud that I think my door's going to pop off its hinges.

I'm not surprised the cops have shown up, but I am a little disappointed. Aren't phoned-in murder tips supposed to be, you know, *anonymous?*

Because I don't want to be involved. I don't want my name in a report. I just want to be a good citizen, even if I spend my days locked away from the general population.

"Ms. Celano?" one of them asks, butchering my surname. It's *sell-AHH-no,* but this one, weirdly, is asking for "Miss Kell-AYE-no."

I look through the peephole at both cops, and the glass morphs their bodies in carnival funhouse dimensions. Big heads, little legs and feet.

"We're here about your phone call," one of them says. "Can you open the door, please?"

My hand rests on the lock and I take a deep breath. I can't remember the last time someone's actually set foot in my apartment. Whenever there's a delivery, I accept it in the relative safety of the building's hallway. If I look through the security doors and feel uneasy, I simply head back inside my apartment.

But where can I hide from these guys? My tiny bathroom?

"Miss Kell-AYE-no?"

"Uh, one minute please!"

I take another deep breath then flip the lock and open the door. The two cops slowly make their way inside, their eyes expertly scanning the interior of my apartment. I wonder what they are thinking. Perhaps they're looking for telltale signs of crazy?

"You're Miss Kell-AYE-no?"

"It's Celano," I say.

"I'm sorry?" the taller of them says.

"Apology accepted."

My peephole view didn't prepare me for the sight of these two land monsters in the flesh. The tall one is seriously tall. He's at least six three, but has a baby face that he tries to hide with a little chin scruff. He would be sort of adorable if I weren't terrified of him and everything he represented.

His partner is almost as tall, and is also nearly double his width. He had to practically step through my doorway sideways.

All of which makes my studio apartment feel all the more claustrophobic. As they look around, I see the place through their eyes and I'm ashamed. My entire world is a dark box subdivided into a tiny galley kitchen, a bathroom, a messy living room with a desk shoved into the corner, and a loft space where I sleep on a single twin mattress. One look at this place and you'd agree: I'm pretty much failing at being an adult.

Baby Face, whose name tag reads YATES, tries to hide his amusement. "Can you tell us what you saw?"

"There was a lady who shot an arrow at a man down by the old viaduct," I say. "And now he's dead."

I basically sound exactly like Dr. Seuss. All I can say, in my defense, is speaking to a person in real life, with my actual voice, is not something I do very often.

"Exactly where was this, ma'am?"

"You know, the viaduct, by Callowhill Street. The old train tracks?"

Yates glances over at his partner, whose nametag reads SEARS, just like the company that makes huge appliances. In fact, this guy reminds me of one of them. I wonder if he comes with a warranty.

"So you were over there with them?" Yates asks. "Or were you just walking by?"

"Neither, I…uh…." And here's what I was dreading. The part where I incriminate myself in the process of trying to do the right thing. I force myself to spit it out. "I saw them from the camera feed from my drone."

"Your camera on *what?*" Sears asks, speaking at last.

"Um, my drone. I use it to look at the city. I was flying it down by the library when I saw two people on the viaduct, which you never see—"

"A drone?" Sears asks.

Yates taps his partner on the shoulder. "You know, man, those flying things kids send up by remote control, to shoot videos from the sky."

Sears finally gets it, which only makes things worse. "So basically, you spy on people?" he asks, leveling a frosty glare at me.

"No, I don't—I swear, I just look at the city."

The cops look at each other with a "get a load of this" expression on their faces. Even *I* know I'm lying. So I give them a brief rundown of my medical history, which is none of their business. They look at me like I'm crazy, and then, as if I hadn't said anything, they continue.

"Those things are a public nuisance," Sears says. "I'm sure your neighbors don't appreciate you looking through their windows or into their backyards."

"I think my neighbors would be more concerned about the crazy lady who's been walking around killing people with arrows!"

Officer Yates sighs. "Look, we checked the viaduct. There's nobody over there. No signs of anything."

"I'm telling you, I saw a woman. She was maybe in her late forties or early fifties. She pulled up her sleeve and..."

"A lot of homeless congregate there. You're looking down at the scene through your computer—"

"Through my cell phone."

"Yeah? Even worse. I think your eyes were playing tricks on you."

Sears interrupts. "Where's this camera drone now?"

"It crashed."

"Into what?"

"Um, it impaled itself on a sign on top of a building."

"So," Yates says, "if we pull the camera out of it, we should be able to see what you saw, right?"

"No," I tell them. "It only transmits live."

"Look, lady," Yates says, handing me his card, "Take my information. If you have something concrete to give us, give me a call. Because unless you have some sort of tape…"

"But my drone doesn't have any recorded footage."

"So in other words," Sears says, "you don't have any proof."

CHAPTER 8

Target Diary–Day 8

IN THE EARLY dawn hours Friday morning I patrol the length of the Parkway, searching for Subject Number Five.

"Would you like some lunch?" I ask. "Blessings to you."

I pull a rolling suitcase behind me. It is full of dry socks, bottled water, soap, toothpaste, and other sundries. Each item is gathered in an individual plastic Ziploc bag to make them easier to dispense.

I also have packed individual lunches. Turkey and cheese on wheat, as well as tuna salad for the individuals who are missing too many teeth. Each sandwich is paired with condiment packets and a small treat, such as a shortbread cookie.

"Are you hungry? Blessings to you."

I am posing as the Ultimate Do-Gooder, selflessly giving up her busy morning to tend to the needs of the less fortunate here in the nation's birthplace.

It only took me a few days to establish this pattern and achieve a level of acceptance among the indigent population.

The police have an unofficial understanding with the homeless here on the Parkway. You can stay after 10 p.m., when the museums are closed, but you have to move to somewhere that's out of sight by 7 a.m.

So I do my hunting on the tail end of that curfew, as the unwashed masses stretch out the stiffness in their limbs and seek their daytime shelter.

"Would you like a lunch bag? Can I give you some clean socks?"

All morning long.

As I pull my bag, I match their pace and try to engage them in conversation so I can look them in the eye. This is vital to my operation. I'm looking for that flicker of hope, that small spark of intelligence. Any small amount of fuel that I can use.

That said, I also don't want someone who can look directly into my eyes. Some of the sheep are very adept at spotting a wolf, and those are the ones to be avoided at all costs.

But as I search and hand out gifts this morning, I can't help but be distracted. The mysterious buzzing sound from yesterday continues to trouble me. I find my eyes flicking skyward at odd moments, as if expecting judgment from somewhere above.

When my eyes were squinting at the sun—did I see something moving through the air? Or was that a figment of my imagination? Or was it simply a benign floater in my field of vision?

"Yo, can I have a tuna?"

"Yes, of course."

My instant kill rate, only fifty percent, also concerns me. I thought I'd have the technique to my wrist apparatus more finely tuned at this point in my mission. Ordinarily I would go days between experiments, because nothing draws the attention of law enforcement like a pattern.

All of these thoughts are leaving me anxious. I need to perfect my art as soon as possible. I expected the practice period to require no more than five subjects, but I might be forced to go as high as nine or ten.

"Are you hungry? Blessings to you."

CHAPTER 9

I WAKE UP early Friday morning and instantly feel depressed.

There's no more *Amelia* to fly around. No way to fly next to my neighbors during their Friday morning commute. No way to check in on my city. I'm trapped in this box of an apartment. I have nothing to look forward to except an e-mail from my German bosses, telling me to restructure my current marketing campaign. Then I'll probably get one from the California bosses that tells me to ignore the Germans, while the Scottish bosses tell me *Aye, ignore the both of them.*

Even when I hear the telltale *clomp-clomp-clomp* of the hot guy from 3-D coming down the stairs, I can barely rouse myself from my mattress and go spy on him through the peephole.

But yeah. I'm *that* depressed.

As much as I hate to admit it, *Amelia* is a goner. I can't very well venture out to pry her off that rusty sign. Nor can I ask any friends (not that I have any of those left, anyway) to go up there and retrieve her for me. That'll result in too many questions and too much awkwardness.

I've come to accept that friends are best kept in the virtual world. The ones I used to have in real life pushed too hard. They didn't understand. I suspect that deep down, they thought I was making all of this up.

Pity party, table for one? Right this way, Ms. Celano!

Geez, even my inner voice feels sorry for me.

There's only one thing that will get me out of this funk this morning. And that's going online and searching for a replacement drone.

Amelia would have wanted it that way.

After about an hour of surfing and browsing and comparing clips on YouTube, I fall in love all over again.

Hello, *Amelia II,* you gorgeous thing.

The new girl is a bit more expensive. Okay, a *lot* more expensive: six hundred bucks. But my would-be *Amelia II* has a better flying range—up to a mile!—and twenty-three glorious minutes of flying time. Best of all, the camera comes with about an hour's worth of on-board memory. When I hit Record, she'll make a movie and then fly it back home to me.

You were looking for proof? I've got your proof *right here,* Officer Sears.

Ordering her with same day delivery will also be a minor shock to the bank account. But what am I supposed to do? Wait until midday tomorrow? By that time, who knows how many other victims "Mrs. Archer" (yeah, that's what I've started calling her) will have racked up. With any luck, *Amelia II* will arrive before sundown, and if set her up quickly, I might be able to squeeze in a quick lap of dusk patrol.

I click BUY NOW.

While I wait for *Amelia II* to show up, I try to do some honest-to-goodness detective work. If I don't know the identity of the killer, maybe I can work an angle from the side of the victim—the one who doesn't even exist, according to Officers Yates and Sears.

One thing I've learned living life online is that there's an advocacy group for everything. And sure enough, there's a Facebook group of concerned neighbors who look out for the homeless around Spring Garden and along the Parkway. I join the group and begin to type:

> Hi everyone! I'm a fellow Spring Garden resident (20th and Green) and I'm worried about a gentleman I used to see along the Parkway.

Already I'm lying. But I don't want to invent too much detail, lest I rule someone out. For instance, I can't say that he's someone I used to joke with, because what if the murder victim had no sense of humor? What if he never spoke at all? So I stick to physical description.

> He's in his late 50s, with longish blond/gray hair and a very long beard. Last time I saw him he

> (Had an arrow sticking out of his chest, and was pleading for his life.)

was wearing a tweed jacket, chinos and wasn't wearing any shoes. I'm worried something may have happened to him. If anyone knows his name

(Because that's what I'm really after.)

or knows where he might be,

(Even though, sadly, I already know this.)

please let me know? Many thanks!

I hit POST and wait for the glorious internet to help me fill in the blanks.

CHAPTER 10

IT'S HARD TO stay focused on work because I can't take my mind off the poor homeless guy, especially now that I've conjured him up in my mind again. Maybe he's someone's missing parent, brother, or husband, and no one in the world (well, except for me) knows what happened to him. Worst of all, I have a feeling that crazy Mrs. Archer has probably killed people many times before, and is preparing to do it again…

Come on, FedEx guy, bring me the goods! The website promises delivery by 8 p.m., but surely you can do better than that?

The afternoon moves forward in a slow, languid crawl. I struggle to check the FedEx tracking site every half hour, instead of every ten minutes. I put on a pair of dark sunglasses and peek out at Green Street from behind my thick drapes. My mom used to say that a watched pot never boils, but that was before the internet. I'm sure there's an app out there that will calculate exactly how many seconds until your water reaches 212 degrees Fahrenheit.

And then finally, at 6:57 p.m., the front door buzzer sounds!

I almost trip as I scramble to the front windows to confirm that the big gorgeous FedEx truck is parked out front on Green, with its blinkers going and all. I know it's probably seriously angering everybody behind him already.

But…no truck?

My usual MO is to have visual confirmation and then buzz the delivery guy all the way in so that he can walk right up to my door and hand over the package—groceries or whatever—while he remains standing in the hallway. But that initial visual confirmation is key.

Oh man. What do I do? Who else could it be, buzzing at me?

I tiptoe over to my door, take a deep breath, then flip the lock and open it the thinnest of cracks so that I can peer through both sets of front doors, scanning for that familiar black and purple uniform of my usual FedEx guy, Gene.

But instead, I see the red baseball cap of Andre, the main delivery guy from Fairmount Pizza, which is a few blocks away. It's weird to see him, because I didn't order pizza…

But then a shadowy form passes my line of sight. I see the tufts of thick black hair as well as a set of broad shoulders sitting squarely under a fitted gray T-shirt. I'd recognize the back of that head and shoulders anywhere.

Seems the guy from 3-D ordered pizza tonight.

"Sorry, man—I hit the wrong buzzer," Andre says. "For a second there I thought I was bringing this to Tricia."

"Who?"

"Your neighbor? Tricia? The girl right over there in 1-B? Anyway, that's $22.95, buddy."

I die a million deaths pushing my door shut as quietly as I can.

Granted, I've never met the guy from 3-D, never introduced myself. But still it hurts that he's so totally unaware of my existence. *Oh, there's someone living in 1-B?*

After that, time slows to a stop. Somehow, the sun sinks below the horizon, which means that even if my package arrives in the next three seconds, there will be no drone flying tonight. I check the FedEx tracking site obsessively now, hitting refresh every minute or so, as I simultaneously check the local traffic news to see if there's, oh, a FedEx truck on fire on the Vine Street Expressway.

Then, after what seems like an eternity…and at ten minutes until eight exactly…the front buzzer finally rings.

This time it's Gene, and he's here for me.

CHAPTER 11

ON SATURDAY MORNING, *Amelia II* is prepped and ready for liftoff.

Okay, so maybe I was up all night getting her ready. Don't judge me.

She's a lot bigger than I imagined. The photos online made her seem like a stealth predator—but in real life, she's as bulky as a flying *Terminator* robot that hunts and kills human beings.

If the first *Amelia* was a sleek dragonfly, her replacement is a fat armored cicada. Maybe that's the price you pay for the extended battery life, expanded range, and camera with memory.

There's no time to break a mini bottle of champagne over her nose by way of christening, though. She needs to be up and patrolling the streets as soon as possible. I push down my sleeves, pull on gloves, open the rear window, then gingerly place *Amelia II* on the sill.

The first thing I notice after liftoff is that *Amelia II* is a bit slower all around. She doesn't maneuver as flawlessly as her predecessor did, nor can she go zooming down the block like her pants are on fire. But that's okay. I'll just have to learn to compensate with the controls on my phone.

As it turns out, I have plenty of time to learn. Because on that first day, I can't seem to locate Mrs. Archer anywhere, even though I sent *Amelia II* out on a record eight daytime patrols.

Sunday doesn't warrant results, either. I don't even want to tell you how many times I flew my poor girl.

But then on Monday morning…

I almost jump out of my own skin when I see the familiar body shape of Mrs. Archer making her way up 19th Street, right next to Baldwin Park.

"Now where have you been, psycho lady?" I murmur excitedly, tweaking the controls so that *Amelia II* can float down for a closer look.

But that's when the weird thing happens.

Mrs. Archer stops in her tracks *and looks up at me,* and it's as if she's heard me talking.

CHAPTER 12

Target Diary—Day 11

AFTER A WEEKEND of thinking that I've been unduly paranoid, I heard the buzzing sound again. Directly overhead.

At first, I was relieved that I hadn't been imagining things. But immediately after that, I became furious at the intrusion of privacy.

Who, exactly, has been keeping tabs on me?

I am prepared for this encounter. For the past ten days I have taken to wearing my wrist apparatus all day long. I want my body movement to look natural at all times so even the most experienced antiterrorism agents won't look twice at me. I keep an arrow spring-loaded and ready for launch at any given second.

Over the weekend, I have perfected my aim. Subjects Five and Six can attest to that. Well, technically, now they're unable to do just that.

I don't even think Six saw her doom coming. Which I suppose was a small mercy for her.

I was thinking about the vacant look in her eyes when I first heard the buzzing.

I glanced up at the source of the sound and immediately realized what I've been dealing with: an unmanned aerial vehicle. Also known as a personal drone.

Presumably, it's equipped with a camera.

The movements are so hardwired into my nervous system that I'm barely aware I'm making them. I lift my sleeve. Raise my arm. Point my finger at the exact location where I want the arrow to make contact. With the drone, I presume that the main body is its electrical center, and a direct strike will take it out of play.

I squeeze the trigger.

CHAPTER 13

THE SKIN ON my arms suddenly turns to gooseflesh. My phone might as well be a brick in my hands for all the good it's doing.

No! Move! Move! Move!

Amelia II is depending on me to steer her out of harm's way. She is equipped with an emergency button that will instruct her built-in GPS to send her back home immediately. The moment I hit that button, however...

She was struck with an arrow.

I didn't actually see it coming at me, though I did see a vague, fluttery blur. And then the image on my screen rocks, and suddenly we're descending down toward the park. No amount of furious screen-tapping is able to control her altitude nor her pitch.

We're going down—hard.

Amelia II bounces, and suddenly I have a view of the perfect September sky, complete with little fluffy clouds. My poor drone is resting on her propellers, which means that liftoff will be impossible.

"No!" I scream, thumbing the buttons anyway.

Then a face fills the screen. Mrs. Archer. She's even uglier up close and personal. And I swear, it's as if she can see me through *Amelia II*'s camera, and she's scowling at me.

She reaches down with thin, reedy fingers and the video stream goes dead a second later, leaving me to stare at a blank screen.

Then a thought occurs to me.

Oh no…

Can she trace *Amelia II* back to me?

CHAPTER 14

Target Diary–Day 11 (continued)

IF ONLY I could dispatch human beings with the same precision that I take out toy drones.

The pathetic little machine sputtered, and then nose-dived into the green grass lawn. I cleared the distance swiftly, before its owner could dart out from the shadows and reclaim it. If I'm to discover who's been spying on me, I need to trace him through his plastic flying machine.

The camera was staring up at me, so I reached down, covered the lens with my palm, and twisted it until I heard a satisfying snap.

Before I scoop up the machine, however, I check my surroundings. Is my nemesis hiding somewhere behind the bushes? Hobbyist drones do not have too great a range. The controller of this one might be very close, or at the most, only a few blocks away.

No matter. I will unmask my spy soon enough.

I hoist the machine from the ground. It is surprisingly light. The only part of this drone that interests me is the "brain"—the neural center that controls low and high speed settings, along with its GPS unit. Everything else runs on rudimentary mechanics.

I snap off the propellers, limbs, and motors, and then I deposit them into a nearby trash receptacle. They land at the bottom with heavy clunks.

The drone's brain goes into a deep pocket in my jacket.

I take in my surroundings one last time, tempted to shout a taunt to my unseen spy. But such a thing would only gratify my ego, and wouldn't serve the greater mission. As I walk away from the park, the drone's brain knocks against my thigh from inside my pocket.

What if that were my job—to take down human beings and steal their brains? That would add an entirely new level of joy and skill to the process. I think I would relish cracking open their skulls and carefully removing their thinking organs.

Civil War soldiers became quite skilled at trepanning in a battlefield. I'm sure that with the resources available to me, I could develop a technique that would leave law enforcement and other agents of justice utterly befuddled.

Human brains, however, are nothing like a computerized brain. We don't yet have the technology to stimulate the dead synapses and recover the intelligence within.

But this is not a human brain. And with a little bit of probing, the drone's brain will give me everything.

It won't be difficult, especially with my level of expertise. If a device was designed to transmit, then it has no choice but to give up its secrets—namely, the internet protocol address of its user.

Ordinary citizens do not realize how much of themselves they surrender to their little smartphones and tablets and other miracle devices. They happily trade their souls for a tiny bit of convenience. Or worse, a meaningless distraction.

I do not own a cell phone or a computer so I can never be traced. Besides, why would I need my own personal version of such devices when there are so many available for the taking?

The central branch of the Free Library of Philadelphia offers everything I need. It only takes a few minutes of surveillance to pinpoint my target: a doughy man in his mid-forties who is poring over historical tomes with his thin laptop off to his left.

History bores me almost as much as old sporting matches. You already know the outcome. Why not focus your attention on making history? That's my objective here in Philadelphia.

I use a classic distraction technique, bumping into his table with just enough force to send those historical tomes a-tumbling. While the doughy man tries to catch them, I scoop his laptop from the table and immediately make a hairpin turn into the stacks. By the time he realizes what has happened and is shouting for a librarian, who tells him to shush out of reflex, I am already safely hidden in a labyrinth of books.

In another room, I help myself to a stray USB cable. This is as easy as breathing! Then, in another room after that, I connect the drone's hardware to my new laptop and start the hunt.

The owner of this drone hasn't entered any of his personal information yet, but that's fine. The IP address is still in its memory, and I log on to a service I frequently use in order to trace it back to its user.

And that's when I find it.

How nice to meet you, Miss Patricia Celano, of 1919 Green Street, Apartment 1-B. I look forward to making your acquaintance in person.

CHAPTER 15

AFTER I'VE GONE through just about the craziest Monday I've ever had, I'm surprised I'm able to sleep at all.

Following the crash of *Amelia II,* I spent the rest of the day in a horrifyingly manic state, checking the peephole through my front door and putting sunglasses on to take a peek through my front windows.

I'm not saying I was stupid enough to tape my name and address to the body of *Amelia II*—IN CASE I'M SHOT WITH AN ARROW PLEASE RETURN TO PATRICIA CELANO, 1919 GREEN STREET, APT. 1A. HUGE THANKS!—but a smart creep could, like, trace the serial number or something to find out who bought her. Heck, I'll bet someone who's especially determined could go on the so-called dark web and find out how many times I've ordered toilet paper in the last year. Why someone would do this, of course, boggles the mind...but you get my point.

And if Mrs. Archer figures out who I am, then what's to stop her from showing up at my door, knocking, and politely putting an arrow through my eye?

Now you might be saying to yourself, *But Tricia, why don't you call those nice tall policemen and tell them what happened?*

Oh, you mean Yates and Sears, the cops who already think I'm a nutcase? I can imagine that exchange already.

Okay, Ms. Celano, first you tell me that this crazy lady shot a homeless guy with an arrow, and now you're telling me she shot your toy drone? Why would she do that?

Seriously, was it *homeless, too?*

And what if they decided that I needed to be put under a twenty-four-hour psychiatric watch or something? I can just see it now—the rest of the cops in the squad room will snicker and roll their eyes as they watch me attempt to function through the tinted glass.

She says she's allergic to the sun, too—I'm tellin' ya, ya can't make this stuff up!

No, thank you.

It is much preferable to spend the rest of my day in a state of extreme paranoia.

Which I do.

Needless to say, not much work gets done today, either. I seem to be jumping at every single noise outside and checking the peephole and windows every fifteen minutes.

So at bedtime, I find myself on my mattress in the loft, staring at the ceiling and trying to calm myself down. With every noise comes the urge to climb down the ladder and check the peephole and windows, but I command myself to stay put. And let me tell you, there are a *lot* of noises at night.

Eventually, though, I do drift off. At least I think I do. That, or I'm so crazy I'm losing whole chunks of my memory because the next thing I know there's a very loud *CRACK!* at my front window.

If my eyes weren't already open, you can bet they're open now.

What the heck was *that?!*

As if in mocking reply to my panicked mental question, there's another *CRACK!*

And yep, there I am, suddenly sitting up in bed (or, er, on my mattress), doing my best impression of a bat as I try to do some echolocation to pinpoint the origin of that sound.

For a blessed number of moments, there is no sound at all. All of Philadelphia seems to be absolutely quiet. It's as if someone hit the Mute button on the entire world.

And then—

CRACK!

My head spins toward the exact location. The god-awful cracking sound is coming from my front windows.

Could be worse, Tricia. It could be coming from inside *the house…*

I crawl off the mattress and somehow force my trembling hands and feet to navigate the ladder all the way down to the floor. As quietly as possible, I make my way across my apartment in the dark. The glow-in-the-dark clock on my wall tells me it's ten after midnight. Ambient light from outside slices through the edges of my curtains. I would appreciate the spooky *film noir* ambience of it all if I weren't so freaking terrified.

I embark on the same circuit I've done what feels like hundreds of times today: I look through the peephole. Then, I push the curtains aside to check out the empty sidewalk on Green Street.

Only...

It's not empty.

Mrs. Archer is standing there, near the curb, hands in her pockets, looking up at me.

CHAPTER 16

Target Diary—Day 12

HELLO, MISS PATRICIA CELANO.

So good to finally put a face to the name.

I spent the better part of my afternoon reading up on you. You seem to live your entire life online, revealing yourself in bits and pieces through Facebook, Twitter, Instagram, Snapchat, Tumblr, and the like.

So why are you being so shy now, ducking behind the window like a frightened child? When you reveal yourself to the world, you can't be shocked when someone like me looks back at you.

But it's not only the information you willingly gave up to the internet. With a little simple digging, I was able to flesh out a fairly detailed biography. I know it all—your work record, your shopping habits, your tax records. I know all of your friends. Your family. Your neighbors.

I know about your medical condition.

Oh yes, I know all about your poor skin, my dear. Such a pity, being cooped up in that $1,350 a month studio apartment all day long.

I almost feel sorry for you.

But alas, you've stuck the nose of your drone in my business, so now it's time to return the favor.

Don't worry, Miss Celano. You won't really see me again until the very end. And by then, it will be too late to do anything about it.

CHAPTER 17

MY ENTIRE BODY freezes. I squeeze my eyes shut, hoping that this is just my mind playing tricks on me. Perhaps the image of Mrs. Archer outside my window is just some kind of bizarre hallucination because I've completely tired myself out today.

But no. When I dare to look again, Mrs. Archer is still standing there, her beady eyes staring *right up into mine*.

Then she cocks her head slightly, slowly removes a hand from her pocket, and makes a little *tsk-tsk* motion with her thick index finger. As if I've been naughty.

Nope nope nope nope…

I choke back a scream, fall to the floor, and duck my head under the windowsill like a small child who's hiding from the bogeyman. How on Earth did she find me so quickly? And how did she know I'd be looking out of my front windows at this exact moment in the middle of the night?

Calm down, I tell myself.

No, YOU calm down, shouts my inner voice.

Then I remember: those cracking sounds. They were from her! She must have been throwing tiny rocks at my window like a lovesick schoolboy. She was trying to wake me up, draw me to my window so she could get a look at my face…

And now she's seen you.

I feel my heart pound the inside of my rib cage. The muscles in my neck tighten. I'm dizzy and I can't breathe. For a horrible moment I think I'm having a heart attack, and wonder how long it will take for the police to find my dead body. Days? Weeks, even?

Then I realize what I'm actually experiencing, and recognize that it's not cardiac arrest. No, I'm having a good old-fashioned panic attack.

I used to get them a lot back in college, when my condition first appeared, albeit in tiny doses. I used to be the kind of kid who loved being outdoors, playing and cavorting from pretty much the crack of dawn until the sun finally went down for the count. So when I found myself unable to enjoy the fresh air on a regular basis, my subconscious took it very, very badly. Or so said my therapist. *Deep down,* she explained, *you feel like you're being buried alive*. It took many expensive sessions in cool, dark rooms to work my way past that feeling.

And now it was back, big time. Thank you, Mrs. Archer.

My brain splits in two: one half tries to push back the sheer panic, and the other focuses on what to do about the murderous stalker outside. What does she want? Is she just frightening me into silence? If so, then I might as well give her the big thumbs-up as I hold up a sign in my front window: MISSION ACCOMPLISHED.

And that's when I hear the front door of my building open. The sound is unmistakable—the creak of the hinges, the echo through the hall.

Someone is entering my building.

CHAPTER 18

AFTER A FEW deep, collected breaths, I force myself to crawl across the hardwood floor. My heart is still pounding like it's trying to launch itself out of my chest. My throat is constricted so tightly that I might as well be wearing a noose.

Halfway to the door of my apartment, I realize that I'm on the ground because subconsciously I'm afraid Mrs. Archer is going to shoot one of those arrows straight through my window and into my skull.

My target: my front door. Because as difficult as it will be to look through that peephole (hello, arrow!), I can't just hide in my apartment, waiting for death to come knocking.

I *have* to know if it's her out there.

As quietly as I can, I place my palms on the door to steady myself as I get my legs up under me. Then, I rise.

And place my eye to the hole.

And…

It's not Mrs. Archer.

Alert the media! Tricia Celano catches a break!

Instead, it's my handsome dark-haired guy from apartment

3-D, just standing there by the mailboxes, lingering, looking down at his cell phone.

He's probably just returned from a night out with his bros, hoisting a bunch of craft beers over artisanal tacos while listening to some indie band over in Northern Liberties or whatever the heck else it is normal people my age do on a Monday night. And now he's probably checking his texts to see if anyone is still up and carousing about before he decides whether it's worth it to call it quits.

I've fantasized a thousand times about opening the door, propping my elbow on the frame and saying, *Hey, there, how's it going?* But a desire to save myself from a case of terminal embarrassment has prevented me from doing so.

This time, though, I have a very good reason to talk to him.

Before I can talk myself out of it, I yank open the door.

Handsome Guy from 3-D looks up from his phone.

"Hi," I say.

"Hey," he says, with a curious expression on his face. It's hovering somewhere between bewilderment and confusion.

"I have a weird favor to ask," I say.

"Okay..."

"No, I mean it. This is seriously going to sound weird."

The Guy smiles. "No worries. What do you need?"

"Um, when you came in did you see someone standing outside, watching the window to my apartment?"

The look on Handsome Guy's face now turns to complete confusion, which makes my thudding heart slam to a halt. There, I've gone and done it. I've freaked him out.

But he quickly recovers and flashes a smile that resuscitates me. "Let me go take another look. I'll be right back."

As he moves back through the vestibule, I pray that I haven't just sent him to his death. That would be one hell of a story to share with the police.

Girl meets boy, boy meets girl, boy gets an arrow in the eye socket for his trouble.

CHAPTER 19

"THE COAST IS clear," he says. "Who did you think was out there?"

"Nobody," I say out of reflex.

"So you wanted me to look outside for you on the off-chance that someone *might* be watching your front windows?"

"I don't know...maybe I was dreaming it, but I thought I saw someone out there. I'm really sorry to have bothered you."

But of course I know this isn't the truth. At this point, I'm sure my eyes weren't lying.

Handsome Guy gives me the same kind of smile you'd give a lost toddler. "You sure you're okay?"

My nerves are so fried at this point that I say a few words that I immediately want to suck back into my mouth and swallow. "No, I really don't think so."

Argh, what are you doing, Tricia?

But Handsome Guy turns out to be the extremely chivalrous type. He gently steers me back into my own apartment and closes the door and guides me to the couch and sits me down and then places himself a friendly, yet respectful, distance away.

"It's okay. Everything's going to be fine," he says. "Look, my name's Jackson—"

"Dolan," I blurt out, because of course I know his name. The moment I realized he lived in 3-D, I took a peek at a package waiting for him in the hallway one time. *Jackson Dolan.* Of course he'd have a cool name like Jackson Dolan. (And don't think I didn't try that surname on for size. Tricia Dolan. It has a nice ring to it, don't you think?)

Jackson raises his eyebrows in surprise.

"Sorry," I say. "I'm a bit of a snoop. Anyway, I'm Tricia..."

"Celano," he says with a grin. "Guess that makes us both snoops."

No, that makes my heart swell three times its normal size. Jackson Dolan actually knows who I am! That means, at one point, he wondered who I was, and peeked at my mail, too. Or maybe he even asked around....

"Tell me what's going on," Jackson says. "I'm a big boy, I can take it."

I want to gush and tell him everything. My *Amelia*s. Mrs. Archer and her killer arrows. The homeless people she's probably killed. And the fact that she learned my name and address, all thanks to *Amelia II*.

But...I can't. I mean, I can't even believe I'm talking to him! That he's actually here, sitting right on my couch. It's almost surreal, as if a leading man in a movie just removed himself from his two-dimensional prison and stepped down through the television screen to speak to...*me*.

I guess that's what happens when you look out at life through peepholes and computers. The few things you actually encounter in life feel glaringly real.

"It's okay," he says, reaching out and taking my hand. Geez, even his hands are warm and large. They're like no other hands I've seen before. Then again, I haven't been touched by another human being in years, so…

So I tell him.

Everything.

My *Amelias*. Mrs. Archer and her killer arrows. The homeless people she's probably murdered—and so on, and so on. The events of the past few days tumble out of my mouth in non sequiturs. I'm positive they only make sense to me—and that's the problem, right? I'm the only one in the world who believes that Mrs. Archer exists, and that she's doing horrible things to people.

Jackson, to his credit, takes it all in like a perfect gentleman. And when he's finished processing everything, an excited look washes over his face.

"So…you're hunting a killer?"

"I guess that's one way of putting it."

"That. Is. Awesome."

CHAPTER 20

HELLO, *AMELIA III*.

I shouldn't be dropping this kind of money on you, but as Jackson said…I *am* hunting a killer. And what is an amateur housebound sleuth without her magical flying machine?

(I wonder if Nero Wolfe would have kicked Archie Goodwin to the curb if he had an *Amelia* in his life.)

I have to say, it was Jackson's enthusiasm last night that inspired me to keep up with this investigation. Not only did he convince me that I wasn't crazy, but he said that I could actually do something about Mrs. Archer. Like, catch her doing her creepy things with her arrow-shooting device. Maybe even record it this time.

Hence, *Amelia III.* Unlike her older sisters, this sprightly young thing has better maneuvering capabilities in order to avoid those lethal arrows. And I'm going to be able to record everything she sees right on my phone, including (hopefully) Mrs. Archer stalking those poor homeless guys.

How's *that* for proof, Officers Yates and Sears?

Such advances come with a hefty price—not counting the extra money I'm spending for same-day (by 5 p.m. guaranteed!) delivery. But the second fee is also for a good reason: Jackson said he'd stop by right after work so he could learn how to pilot her, too.

Only *I* could turn the hunt for a serial killer into a...*date.*

With all of the dough I'm spending, you'd think I'd be putting my nose to the grindstone at work. *Au contraire, mon frère.* All I can think about is the image of Mrs. Archer, looking up at me from the sidewalk. And Jackson, of course. The one person who doesn't think I'm completely bonkers. Yet.

Somehow I resist the urge to don sunglasses and a knit cap to take a peek out from behind my curtains every seventeen seconds. No good could possibly come of that. (Especially if she's standing out there...*waiting*...and *tsk-tsking* at me.) Maybe that's why the afternoon drags on like a small eternity. Seriously, no day has ever lasted this long before.

And then, finally, both things I've been waiting for happen almost at once.

Amelia III arrives in the afternoon, and she's barely out of the box before there's a knock at my door.

"Is that her?" Jackson asks, excitedly.

"Well, she's indisposed at the moment," I tell him, "but yeah, it's her. Jackson, meet Amelia the Third. Amelia, meet our upstairs neighbor, Jackson."

We dig into the scattered pieces of *Amelia III* like kids on Christmas morning who've received a new Lego set. Jackson reads me the instructions, while I do the snapping and screwing and connecting, all of which is cake for me now. The two of us have the easy groove of a married couple putting together a crib.

The whole evening is shocking to me because I've known Jackson less than twenty-four hours, and I rarely have contact with other human beings. Especially startling is my ability to banter with him.

"I hope you're not afraid of heights."

"Why?"

"Because if I crash *Amelia III* on a roof, I'm going to need somebody to climb up and get her for me."

Jackson chuckles. "Well, how about we don't crash her then?"

"We? You think I'm actually going to put my girl in the hands of a complete stranger?"

"C'mon, we're neighbors."

"Stranger danger, stranger danger..."

But after a brief tutorial, I *do* let Jackson pilot *Amelia III* around the neighborhood. He's quite agile with the controls. ("Years of wasting my life with a PlayStation controller in my hands," he explains.) I love watching his hands. They are lean and strong.

Of course, I'm splitting my attention with the image on my laptop. Jackson helped me figure out how to beam it from my phone to the laptop so I'd have a bigger image of the neighborhood as we go speeding by.

"Any sign of her?"

"Not yet," I say. "Just keep her steady, Captain."

"I'd better bring her back. Amelia's almost run out of her battery life."

"That's because we rushed her out before she had a full charge."

"We were excited."

I'll say we were excited.

Jackson is the first person in a long time who doesn't think I'm a freak. What's he going to think, then, when I'm forced to explain my medical condition to him? Sooner or later, it'll come up. It always comes up.

Only, I'm hoping it doesn't happen too quickly.

That is, until he asks, "After we bring her in for a landing, how about we grab a quick bite? I'm starving."

"Oh, right," I say, clearing my throat nervously. "I guess it is getting late. But you know, I'd better get back to work. I'm kind of behind on a few things, with all of this excitement."

"Are you sure?" Jackson asks. "I know this great café just a block away, on the corner of Green and 21st. My treat, since you let me fly Amelia the Third and everything."

Argh, this is killing me.

"Maybe we could go some other time? I'm really sorry."

Jackson is quiet for a moment, as if he's trying to figure out whether I'm really swamped with work or just not into him. I want to scream, *TRUST ME, I AM TOTALLY INTO YOU!* But of course, I say nothing.

"Sure, maybe some other time," he says.

And it *kills* me.

CHAPTER 21

BUT AFTER JACKSON leaves, I don't throw myself into my actual job. Instead, I resume my online hunt for the name of the murdered homeless man while *Amelia III* recharges. (Unfortunately, her battery's so low that I won't get the chance to fly her again tonight; the sun is already setting.)

I try not to think about the hurt puppy-dog look on Jackson's face as he excused himself from my apartment. Why couldn't I have said something vaguely romantic like, *Hey, why don't I whip up something here for the two of us?* Because I'm an idiot, that's why. We could have shared a meal together, maybe even kept up with some more of that playful banter we had been exchanging.

But no. I had to tell him *maybe some other time.*

Anyway...that's why I'm distracting myself, looking for some news on the homeless advocacy front. I check Facebook, and there's a single message waiting for me from an older hippyish-looking guy named John Burke:

Hello, Tricia. There's a fellow named Allen Moyer who hasn't been seen around the Parkway in a while. (But

I also hear that he might be up visiting a cousin in Wilkes-Barre.)

Things are a little chaotic down at the Parkway anyway; they're preparing for the senator's visit on Wednesday, so they've been shooing people away and putting up barricades like it's a goddamn police state. Chances are, your missing guy was probably one of the unfortunate ones to be shooed away first.

Hope this helps. Blessings to you.

Right back at ya, Mr. Burke.

Of course, this is no lead at all. I was hoping for...I don't know, a set of *actual clues* to go on. It's not as if I can fly *Amelia III* up to Wilkes-Barre (wherever the heck that is) to snoop around the Moyer family. If that's even the right guy at all.

I do a search for "Allen Moyer," but there are no hits anywhere near Philadelphia. An image search brings up a bunch of white dudes, mostly in goatees, who look nothing like the man I saw that day.

So I type Mr. Burke a reply:

Thanks so much for your help, Mr. Burke! At the risk of pressing my luck...do any of your contacts have a description of Mr. Moyer? Or, by chance, a photograph? I want to be sure I'm thinking of the same man. Huge thanks, and blessings to

My message is interrupted by a knock at the door.

First thought: it's Jackson, with flowers and take-out because he couldn't stand the idea of dining without me.

Hah.

Second thought: aside from *Amelia III,* I didn't have any deliveries scheduled for today. (And when you're stuck inside, your life kind of revolves around deliveries.)

Weird.

But then comes my third, and most chilling thought: *Mrs. Archer has returned.*

And now she knows that I'm alone.

Instantly, my heart is pounding and my throat is tightening and my brain feels like it's swimming in my head. No. Not again. I refuse to turn into a basket case for the second time in a twenty-four-hour period. I go to the front door and look through the peephole and—

Nobody's there.

But there is movement behind the shades of my front window. I quickly put on my sunglasses and knit cap and peek outside, just in time to see a bright green Fresh Grub Now truck parked outside, near the corner. Which is one of my delivery services. Did I have something scheduled for today? Could I have simply forgotten?

Back at the door, I take a deep breath, then flip the lock and twist the knob. Sure enough, there's an insulated Fresh Grub Now bag waiting for me.

The bag is small, but heavy. Why would I have placed such a small order? That's just a waste of the delivery fee.

I bring the bag to the kitchen, drop it on the counter, and pull out the contents. They seem to be a dense squishy mass of...*something*. Then the odor hits me. It takes me a while to place, because I'm vegetarian. And even when I was a preteen and still eating meat, my parents always opted for the fresh stuff.

But that's not what this is.

This is rotten meat.

CHAPTER 22

IT'S NOT A THREAT.

It's not a threat.

It's not a threat.

I tell myself.

But honestly, what else could it be? *Oops, looks like I clicked on the wrong box at the website. I meant to check "rhubarb treat," not "rotten meat"!* I check my order history, and discover that, of course, I didn't order any food from Fresh Grub Now in the past few days.

No, this little package must have been a gift from you-know-who.

I know I'll have fat luck, though, convincing Officers Yates and Sears that this huge chunk of fetid meat was from my friendly neighborhood murderer. It's not like my track record is working in my favor in that department.

I hastily rewrap the meat in the Fresh Grub Now bag and consider walking it straight to the dumpster behind the building… except, I *never* walk to the dumpster. (My landlord takes pity on me and allows me to leave my lonely little trash and recycling outside my door every Monday, and he takes it out from there.)

So I have no choice but to leave this disgusting chunk of decaying meat in my trash bin all week. Which is going to be awesome.

Maybe it's psychosomatic, but as the evening goes on, the smell of that meat becomes even more intense. For a moment, I consider putting it out in the hallway anyway. But then the odor would waft throughout the building. I'm sure that'd turn me into everyone's least favorite tenant in about two hours flat.

Even if Jackson were to come knocking at my door right now, flowers in hand, I'd have to turn him away before he started gagging.

I spray the living daylights out of the interior of my trash bin with a bathroom deodorizer before I go to bed. If I had a hundred of those pine tree car fresheners, I'd hang them all over my apartment, just like that crazy guy did in the movie *Se7en*. Honestly, anything would be better than this.

My mind is too agitated to allow itself to sleep. I keep thinking about the meat. And *why* meat? It's kind of a juvenile prank, along the lines of leaving a flaming bag of doggie doo on your doorstep.

Unless...

Unless Mrs. Archer somehow *knew* about my condition. And that I'd essentially be trapped inside this one-room apartment with rotten meat for an entire week. Which makes it downright diabolical.

Crazy Arrow Lady: 1

Tricia: 0

Sometime after midnight I finally drift off, which is a nice break from the stench. I dream about walking around outside. It's a common recurring dream for me. There's fresh-cut grass under my feet, and warm sun on my face, and it isn't covering my skin with blisters or turning it to ash. Maybe my subconscious mind is starved for this experience and recreates it when I'm in my most defenseless state. Or maybe my subconscious just likes to torture me with what I can't have.

But for the moment, it's all so wonderfully real and vivid that I forget about my troubles. Do you remember those carefree days as a kid during the summer, when time seemed to stretch into forever? No homework, no responsibilities whatsoever? That's what this dream felt like, right up until the moment—

My front door slams shut.

CHAPTER 23

I'M SCRAMBLING DOWN from my sleeping loft before I'm even fully awake, slamming my elbows into walls and banging my knees on the ladder. I'm in such a hurry that I don't realize that I'm doing something very stupid.

What if the slamming door was meant to wake me up, and right now I'm rushing into the waiting, murderous arms of Mrs. Archer?

I skid to a halt in the middle of my apartment and attempt to see in the near dark. Is there someone in here with me?

If there were an intruder, Tricia, what exactly would you do about it?

The heart, the throat, the brain—they all start up again with the pounding, the tightening, the dizziness. Instead of paralyzing me, though, the panic attack seems to spark the opposite effect. I'm suddenly furious.

"Is there somebody here?" I say. "Look, if there's someone in this apartment, stop being a coward and show your face!"

There is no reply. The gloomy dark keeps its own counsel.

One by one, I flip on the lights, illuminating every square inch of my place. One by one, potential hiding spots are eliminated.

After a good fifteen minutes of searching (it's not a big place—but I searched everything five times anyway), I'm reasonably sure I am alone.

But I am definitely awake. There will be no more sleeping tonight.

I consider calling Jackson, who's probably sleeping just two floors above me. But no, he doesn't need my brand of crazy in his life right now. I'll just have to deal.

I spray the inside of the trash bin with deodorizer again, but it doesn't seem to do anything. I don't think the fetid stench will ever get out of my nostrils.

I'm still angry. So, somewhere around 4 a.m. on Wednesday morning, I silently tell Mrs. Archer:

You psycho—it's time for me to take the fight to you.

CHAPTER 24

I'M READY BEFORE the crack of dawn on Wednesday morning. *Amelia III* is perched on my windowsill and ready for active duty. Let's do this thing.

Amelia III flies up, up, up, and over the edges of my rooftop. Then she zooms toward the city proper. This is my first time piloting her, since Jackson had the honors of making the maiden voyage. And *wow,* is she a thing of beauty. No offense to the previous *Amelias*, but they were basically just radio-controlled helicopters when compared to this fighter jet of a drone.

I swoop around the Parkway. Today there are wooden barricades, all up and down the sides of the street, which means Philly will be hosting some kind of important visitor this afternoon. Then I remember: it's the senator that Mr. Burke mentioned. That's the reason the authorities shooed all of those homeless people away.

But never mind that. I need to focus on my target.

I check Mrs. Archer's last known locations, hoping she's returned to the scene of the crime. I start in the park, but there's no sign of her there. So I guide *Amelia III* down 19th Street and I'm about to enter the viaduct when I see…

Flashing lights.

Police—and they're like, *everywhere*.

What's going on?

The tricky thing here is getting a good view without the police knowing that I'm watching. Fortunately, they're so busy keeping onlookers on the fringes of the scene that none of them even bother to look up. (Besides, it definitely helps that *Amelia III* is much quieter than her sisters.)

I tweak the controls until I'm at the best vantage point possible, allowing me to see right down into the viaduct, where there is a lot of activity and uniforms and detectives and forensic-type people.

My blood freezes as I realize what the police are doing.

They're carrying dead bodies away from the scene.

The urge to vomit almost overpowers me—and not just because there's a stench of rotten meat in my apartment.

I struggle to keep *Amelia III* steady as I count the bodies under the tarps.

There are *six* of them.

Apparently, Mrs. Archer has killed many people.

Was the murder I saw the first one? Do I share the blame for those five other poor souls? Did they die because I'm such a freak and wasn't able to convince two police officers that what I saw was real?

This isn't happening. This can't be happening…

My view of the crime scene is interrupted by a ding on my cell phone—a Facebook message is waiting for me.

It's from John Burke, the homeless advocate who messaged me

last night. No doubt he's heard about the bodies being discovered and checking in to see if I know anything.

I know more than you could ever guess, Mr. Burke…

I hesitate clicking on the message, though—what am I supposed to say? That I knew what was happening all along and wasn't able to stand up and do anything about it?

Stop being a baby. Answer the man's message.

But it's not a Facebook message from John Burke at all. Instead, it's a dark, slightly blurry photograph from an unknown account. What the hell?

I use my thumb and middle finger to pinch it open.

And I see it's an image of me.

Sleeping in bed, nearly eight hours ago.

CHAPTER 25

Target Diary–Day 13 (The Big Day)

SOMETIMES YOU THINK a mission is all nailed down. You've planned every detail to perfection. Every possible scenario is conjured and considered.

And then along comes a wrench. Or in this case, a nosy little *wench,* who throws herself into the works. Now a dilettante would react to such a complication with panic or, at least, fear of discovery. Most likely, the final result would be a cowardly abandonment of the mission.

But, as I've explained before, I am no dilettante.

The mark of a truly gifted operative is to take those frustrating little complications and work them into the very fabric of your mission. Not only will your antagonist never see it coming, but if you're smart enough, it will seem like the complication was part of the mission all along.

And how exciting, this new adjustment to the mission!

The first thing I did was shake Miss Patricia with a special delivery. I couldn't have her get too cocky and comfortable.

The police discovered the bodies of Subjects One through Six exactly as I'd planned. It happened the day after I visited the pit, taking the piece that I needed with me. Then I phoned in the anonymous tip myself.

And then, posing as "John Burke," I reached out to my dear Patricia so I could give her a little bit of comfort about her mysterious homeless man. After all, for my plan to work, I can't have her become too unhinged. Now, I need her to fall asleep.

Patricia Celano, I hope you understand. We were meant to be joined together on this wonderful day. It's almost as if you and your particular affliction were crafted by some brilliant deity for this singular purpose. My purpose.

Blessings to you.

CHAPTER 26

THERE'S NO TIME for a panic attack. I barely have time to pilot *Amelia III* back home safely before there's a sharp *knock-knock-knock* at my door.

Please don't be Mrs. Archer, come to finish me off…

But no. The view through the peephole reveals the burly frames of Officers Yates and Sears. And this time, I couldn't be happier to see them. I fling open the door, feeling like my soul has just lost three hundred pounds.

"If you're here to apologize, then you're in luck. Because I'm taking apologies all morning long."

Yates, the babyface, says, "I'm sorry?"

"Ms. Celano, we're here to ask you a few questions," Sears says. "May we step inside?" He asks the question without really requesting my permission.

"Sure, come on in. Want me to put on some coffee?"

Yates wrinkles up his nose. "Ugh, what is that smell?"

"The garbage. Which is part of the reason I'm so happy to see you guys. You won't believe what's been going on the past couple of days."

"So you've been inside your apartment this whole time?" Sears asks. "You never left once?"

"No. I haven't," I say. "Like I explained to you the other day, I have this..."

"Sun allergy, right," Sears says. "I did some looking into that. It's extremely rare. I mean, like, you'd have a better chance of being struck by lightning while winning the lottery."

"I guess that's me," I say. "Lady Luck."

Yates and Sears give each other a knowing look. What is going on with these two?

"Look, I'm not the type to say I told you so, but I saw the news about all the bodies you guys found."

"You did?" Yates asks.

"Yeah. I swear to God, though, I only knew about the one! The one I told you about. I don't know if she's been at this a while, or racked up a few more since I last saw you guys, but—"

Sears interrupts, "How many bodies did you hear we found?"

"Six."

"And how, exactly, did you hear about them?"

"What do you mean?"

"TV? The radio?" Yates asks. "Maybe online?"

And that's when I realize I've been caught in a lie.

"Because, you know, the department hasn't released any details to the media yet," Sears says.

"Okay, I admit it," I say, huffing out a breath. "I flew my drone over the scene and saw what was going on. And I swear, I was about to call you guys when I heard from the killer again. She was here! Inside my apartment last night!"

"Hold on—what drone?" Sears asks. "I thought you said you crashed that drone after you saw this supposed killer."

"Unless you left the apartment at night to take the drone you crashed off the roof," Yates says. "Is that what happened? Were you able to get it back and fix it?"

They're both trying to catch me in a lie. I already said I hadn't left the apartment in days—so why would I admit to slipping out at night (which I haven't)? Why would they do such a thing?

Oh no, I realize.

They think I did it.

CHAPTER 27

"LOOK," I TELL THEM. "I know how this is going to sound, but I need you guys to believe me."

Sears gives me this super-patronizing smile. "Why don't you tell us what happened, and we'll let you know how your story sounds?"

Thing is, I know *exactly* how it sounds. But I try to clear my name anyway.

"So I bought another drone—you know, because I crashed the first one."

"We remember," Yates says. "And like I said, did you ever manage to pull it down from the roof?"

"No, dummy, she *can't,* because she's allergic to *the sun,*" Sears says, with all of the conviction of a man telling another man that the Easter Bunny is real.

"Anyway," I say, "this drone had recording capabilities. That way, if I found Mrs. Archer—"

"Who?" Sears asks.

"That's what I've been calling the suspect. You know, because of the arrow thing? I wanted to capture Mrs. Archer on film so I'd finally have proof for you guys."

"That's very nice of you," says Yates. "So did you find her?"

"Um, yes and no. I definitely caught her, in the park down on 19th Street."

"So let's see the footage."

"Well…I can't because she shot my drone out of the sky with an arrow."

Both tough guy cops blink at that one.

"I'm sorry?" Yates asks.

"I don't know what to tell you, other than the fact that she has amazing aim. But yeah, she took down my drone with an arrow, then presumably destroyed it, which is why I don't have any footage of her."

"You said she shot it down…with an arrow?"

This is getting annoying. "Can we move past the arrow? Please? Because the really scary thing is that I think she traced my address and online identity through the drone. And now some really weird things have been happening to me over the past couple of days…"

Then I start to gush, telling them about everything—the rocks against my window pane in the middle of the night and the delivery of rotten meat. Everything except my new visits with Jackson Dolan, because the last thing I want to do is send these two lugs to his front door. I may be a freak who has to hide indoors all the time, but I'm not the girl who brings trouble into someone else's home.

And that's when I suddenly remember the creepy sleeping photo.

"Oh, wait! I do have proof."

Officer Yates makes this grand sweeping gesture as if to say, *Well, then lead us to it, my fair lady.*

I open my laptop then call up Facebook. There it is—the message, and the photo of me taking forty winks. "See? Clearly I couldn't have taken this."

I sense the sheer presence of their bodies as they both lean around me to take a look at the image. Not only do I not come in close proximity to any other human beings 99 percent of the time, but I never have this kind of personal space violation. My heart begins to do its jackrabbit thing and my throat tightens.

"You know, a friend could have easily taken that," Yates says.

"What kind of friend would sneak into my place and snap a photo of me while I'm sleeping?"

"The kind of friend who wants to help you create an alibi," Sears says.

There's a truly awful moment where I think the handcuffs are going to come out. I'll be read my Miranda rights, but it won't matter, because the moment they drag me outside this building will be the moment my heart explodes, and my skin disintegrates to nothing.

CHAPTER 28

HELP ME, *AMELIA III*, you're my only hope.

Up she goes, clearing my rooftop and gliding over Spring Garden, making a beeline for the Parkway. Even though my girl has enough battery power to last for a long and leisurely flight, my own clock is ticking. I need proof of Mrs. Archer's existence, and I need it now.

Otherwise, I might be facing a long stretch of time in an even smaller room.

The image on my cell phone—beamed straight from *Amelia III*'s camera—reveals a strangely busy Parkway. There are throngs of people lining the sidewalks, with police vehicles and ambulances and concessions and oh crap...that's when I remember. The political rally!

Being the completely self-absorbed millennial I am, I don't follow politics like I should. But after that weird e-mail from Mr. Burke (blessings, indeed) I looked up an article about this senator and his visit to Philadelphia.

Turns out he's not just a senator from Utah—he's the vice-presidential nominee after the guy they had announced over the summer suffered from a complete meltdown and had an embarrassing flame-out (as they sometimes do).

So now Senator Dude from Utah is making the lightning rounds around the country, trying to introduce himself to everyone in enough time for the November election. This afternoon, he's making a stop in the City of Brotherly Love.

And *Amelia III* has the perfect point of view to watch the main event.

There's no hiding from me, Mrs. Archer.

That is, until *Amelia III* reaches the fringes of the Parkway. The view on my phone goes all jittery, as if she's had a pre-flight shot of vodka.

"What are you doing?" I mutter.

The controls under my thumbs are suddenly useless. I can't adjust the pitch or altitude or *anything*. This doesn't make any sense! Come on, girl—what are you doing up there?

Suddenly *Amelia III* turns to show me the crowd below, and then we're rushing toward it. Like, at supersonic speed. No, no, no—not toward the people! My thumbs pound on my cell phone so hard I'm shocked the screen doesn't shatter.

Thankfully, *Amelia III* rights herself at the last minute and swoops right over the rally-goers, heading for an expanse of green. And then, rather unceremoniously, she crashes into a line of trees near the Barnes Foundation.

My screen is full of swirling leaves and branches as she tumbles down through the thick trees. I have no idea what the heck just happened. Did Mrs. Archer spot my girl before I spotted *her*, felling my poor drone with another arrow? But that would be crazy, right?

Finally, the leaves clear a bit as *Amelia III* comes to a halt. Her camera is pointed down at the sidewalk, where a group of rally-goers are gawking up at us.

Hi, hello, nothing to see here, folks.

But then the crowd parts and men in dark suits with plastic earpieces come running up. One of them is holding a device that looks like one of those radar guns the police use to catch speeders on the highway. Another one is pointing up at us—that is to say, at my poor *Amelia III*.

The radar gun looks familiar, but where have I seen it before?

I scramble to my coffee table where there's a messy pile of magazines (don't judge—even a housebound, sun-allergic girl needs her hits of high fashion). Under a stack of *Vogue*s, I find it—a UK magazine called *Drone Life*. That could actually be the title of my autobiography. But I digress…

Flipping through the pages like a maniac, I finally find it. That wasn't a radar gun, and it wasn't meant to track speed. The thing is an anti-drone gun, designed to disable an aircraft like *Amelia III*.

Holy cats—*Amelia III* must have been taken down by the US Secret Service!

I guess they have a zero tolerance policy when it comes to visiting senators and private flying aircrafts.

Meanwhile, onscreen, I'm treated to the sight of a G-man climbing the tree toward *Amelia III,* as if she's a frightened kitten in need of rescue. This would ordinarily amuse me, except for a few sad truths:

I'm no closer to finding Mrs. Archer or proving she exists.

That was just $1,500—i.e., more than a rent payment—down the drain.

Soon *Amelia III* will be in the possession of the Secret Service, and soon they'll know my name, and soon I should expect the attention (and comic stylings) of Officers Yates and Sears—or worse, the FBI or CIA.

I am so screwed.

CHAPTER 29

LOCATE YOUR CHILL.

That's what my online friends tell me when I freak out about something they feel is trivial. (Like, say, never being able to feel the warm sun on your skin.) *It's going to be okay, Tricia,* they say. *Locate your chill.*

Most of the time, I absolutely *hate it* when my friends tell me to locate my chill.

It kind of makes me want to locate my inner rage and drop it on them like a nuclear bomb.

Nonetheless, I try to follow that advice now and locate my chill. And I do that by trying once again to locate my nemesis—Mrs. Archer.

I hit the homeless advocacy boards on Facebook, seeing if anyone has a fresh lead on my murder victim. (Well, not *my* victim…ah, you know what I mean.) I repost my original description, hoping to catch different pairs of eyes this time. I add a bit more pathos, telling everyone how worried I am about this guy, especially with all of the crowds down by the Parkway.

About a microsecond after I hit the Post button, one of the homeless advocates sends me an instant message:

Why are you asking about this NOW? Haven't you heard what happened?

I blink. What is that supposed to mean? Then, a second later:

It's all over the news!!!

I open a new browser tab and check my favorite local news site (*The Philly Post*) and holy crackers and cheese—I can't believe what I'm reading.

That visiting senator from Utah? That guy who is trying to become our nation's vice-president?

He was just assassinated.

CHAPTER 30

I READ THE breaking news article in a kind of stunned haze, feeling like I was just involved in a car accident. Nonetheless, certain words jump out at me.

woman in crowd.
vanished without a trace.
killed with what appears to be an arrow...

No.

No no no no...

But that's what's being reported. In the middle of cheers and handshakes and a marching band performance of a Sousa march, a middle-aged woman fired an arrow straight into the heart of the good senator from Utah, killing him almost instantly.

Eyewitnesses differ on the description of the assassin, who is said to have disappeared into the throngs gathered on the Parkway...

It all makes sense.

Perfectly horrible sense.

Only now do I realize what Mrs. Archer has been up to this whole time. She's not a serial killer hunting homeless people. They were just *practice* for her main goal. She's been gearing up for something far, far worse...

And I could have stopped her days ago.

I pick up my cell and dial Jackson. All of those rules about waiting a certain number of days before calling a guy have gone right out the window. I'm pretty sure there's a clause about being involved in a political assassination, right?

"Hey! Tricia! How are you?"

He's huffing and puffing, as if he's out of breath.

"Not good, to be perfectly honest, but...I'm sorry, is this a bad time?"

"No, it's fine. Why?"

"You sound like you're climbing the Rocky steps at the Art Museum."

Jackson laughs. "Ah, you caught me. I was just squeezing in a little exercise, and I guess I got winded faster than I thought. Kind of embarrassing. But what's up?"

"You haven't heard the news?" I ask, but then realize that I was very recently accused of not watching the news, either. "Never mind. Mrs. Archer has done something really, seriously horrible, and I think she's trying to pin it on me!"

"Whoa, take it easy."

Girl, if he tells you to locate your chill, you hang up on him.

I choke back my frustration and try to remain calm. "If you saw the news, you'd know that pretty much the last thing on my to-do list right now would be to *take it easy*."

"Then come on upstairs."

The suggestion, simple as it is, stuns me.

"To…your apartment?"

"Yes," Jackson says with a chuckle. "You know the one, right? 3-D. Like the movies."

"I thought you were exercising."

"Yeah, in my apartment. But I just stopped. Look, I'm still panting because I'm not exactly in optimal shape. There, are you happy?"

"I didn't mean to…look, I'm sorry. I should probably go."

"Come on, don't be silly, and just come upstairs. We'll figure this out together."

Together. He says it so casually it makes me fall for him all over again. And before I can protest any further, he hangs up.

But upstairs?

Me?

He's got to be kidding. I haven't even been all the way down my hallway in a couple of years.

Then I remember my predicament. The last place I want to be is in my own apartment, alone, with the Philadelphia Police Department already suspicious of me. Plus the Secret Service about one internet search away from discovering Patricia Celano, the woman behind the drone they've shot down.

I've toughed it out alone all of these years.

Maybe it's time I actually ask for a little help.

CHAPTER 31

I SLIP ON a light jacket and pull the hood up over my head. My hand grabs the knob and turns it. The door creaks open. The hallway looks about a thousand feet long. And beyond them, the ornate wooden staircase looks so foreign to me that it might as well be a detail in an alien spaceship in a sci-fi movie.

Years ago, this was one big brownstone mansion before they divided it up into a bunch of apartments. My prison cell of an apartment was probably only a study or something. I live in a big house and have never seen 95 percent of it.

"Come on Tricia," I say aloud, trying to psych myself up. "There's no reason you can't do this."

Oh yeah? How about the crippling panic attack that will shut down your heart in about ten seconds?

"That's not real. The only thing preventing you from walking upstairs is a delusion."

I'll be sure to mention that to the coroner when he shows up.

This is the debate I have with myself—half out loud, half in my head. At this point, I'm freaking out so much that I'm not even sure which parts are which.

But it's good, because the banter distracts me while my body steps out into the hallway and moves slowly toward the staircase. My feet follow a perfect line, as if someone had laid a tightrope across the floor.

The whole experience—moving down the hallway and ascending the two flights of stairs—is sort of dreamlike. I keep my head down, with my hands in my pockets, my right hand clutching my cell phone like it's something that can protect me during this dangerous journey.

I hear the stairs creak beneath my feet and avoid the rays of sunlight that blast in through side windows. It's a good thing that I'm wearing the hoodie.

The feeling is so bizarre that I wonder if I *am* dreaming all of this, the whole thing. Maybe I'll wake up any minute now in my sad little apartment with my toy drones and realize I've been so starved for human contact that I conjured it all up. Mrs. Archer. The dead homeless guy. The cops. The senator.

Even cute Jackson Dolan. Because in real life, why would a guy like him even bother with a freak like me?

I snap out of my reverie when I reach his door—3-D. The fact I'm actually standing here is unreal.

"Jackson?"

I knock timidly at first, then a little harder. The door opens—just a crack—with the same creaking noise as mine. He left it open for me.

"It's me… Tricia."

I push open the door a little farther and a strange odor fills my nostrils. Ugh. What is that? Post-workout sweat gone horribly wrong? And to think, I was self-conscious about the *eau de rotten meat* in my own apartment.

"Jackson, um, are you still here?"

Brazenly, I push open the door a bit more so I can see the layout of his apartment.

It's just as small and dark as mine, but laid out in a different way. The shades are drawn, so it's hard to make out much detail.

From my vantage point in the hallway, however, I can see all the way through his living room and into his shadowy bathroom, where there is an arm dangling over the edge of a bathtub.

The arm is not moving, and it doesn't appear to be alive.

CHAPTER 32

Target Diary—Day 13 (The Big Day, continued)

THE HARD PART is over. I lean back against a parked car, pull a candy bar from my jacket pocket, carefully rip open one end of its wrapper. Then I peel the plastic back halfway down the bar like it's a banana skin.

The candy bar is a Snickers. I love the combination of nougat and caramel and peanuts, enrobed in a thin shell of chocolate. I take a long leisurely bite, chewing slowly, savoring the sugar rush and marveling at how something that looks so unappetizing on the outside can pack so much delicious flavor inside.

There's only one thing that gives me more pleasure than this Snickers bar. And that's the fact that right about now, Miss Tricia Celano will most likely be doing one of two things.

The first option is that she's cowering in her apartment, waiting for law enforcement to arrive. This would, of course, be a satisfactory way to bring my mission to a successful—albeit humdrum—conclusion. My expectation is that the government investigators haven't considered Miss Celano seriously as a suspect. But her strange condition will inject plenty of doubt into the case, completely obfuscating my involvement in the matter of the slaughtered senator. Even if the government *were* to believe her story, they'd be scouring the country for a middle-aged woman. Which I, certainly, am not.

On the other hand, Miss Tricia Celano could be making her way up to apartment 3-D, where I left the door unlocked. Will she be bold enough to venture inside?

And if so, will she find the present I left her in the bathroom?

Will it make her scream?

Especially when she sees the arrow in the eye, which killed the poor fellow almost instantly?

There's a good chance she'll scream.

But there is a small chance she'll summon some inner strength previously unknown to her and take a good look at the face of the corpse in said bathroom.

And oh, I very much hope she will.

Because upon closer inspection, she may notice that while the details of his face generally resemble the man she's come to know as "Jackson Dolan," they won't exactly match his. I was working off hastily made reconnaissance photographs, and even though I am quite skilled at the art of impersonation, there are some limits to my abilities.

And Miss Celano, if you *do* notice the small discrepancies, what will you do then?

Will you run to the police with your discovery?

Perhaps.

But I'm hoping not.

Because you're special. Because you amuse me.

I realized that the moment you stepped into my life and I

learned everything I could about you. Your skin allergy. Your habits. Even your girlish crushes. You really shouldn't openly fawn over the "handsome guy from 3-D" if you don't want someone like me taking advantage of that particular emotion.

So no, I do not believe you will run to law enforcement.

And besides, I've already called them.

You'll soon realize how inescapable the trap is that I've assembled around you. That you're much like a lab rat who realizes that—if it is to survive—it must abandon the one habitat it has known all of its short, miserable life.

You're a rat, Miss Celano. And you're about to gnaw your way out of your own cage. Which is a good thing.

Because I'll be outside waiting for you.

CHAPTER 33

THERE IS AN arrow sticking out of my dead boyfriend's eye socket.

Yes, I know he's not *technically* my boyfriend, but he's not exactly alive, either. Right now, I just need a minute to come to my senses.

I'm still in shock.

Somehow I find the strength to touch his neck, just to make sure, but his flesh is cold. Very horribly cold. He's been dead a long time. I look at his skin and at the congealed, partially dried blood at the bottom of the tub.

That's when I realize I can't look at him anymore. I take a deep breath and it's a huge mistake. The stench is horrible. Clearly, this happened more than a few hours ago. Most likely, it's been days.

So how did he answer his cell phone just five minutes ago?

Duh, Tricia—this is not the man who talked to you five minutes ago.

So then who the hell is he?

Downstairs, on the first floor, there's a loud banging sound that reverberates like gunfire up the stairwell. It startles the hell out of me. This is followed by the baritone voice of Officer Sears, which startles me even more.

"Ms. Celano! Open up. It's Officer Sears. We need to talk to you."

KNOCK KNOCK KNOCK.

The pounding sounds again.

"We have a warrant, Tricia." This is Yates now. "You don't open up, we're going to come in anyway."

"Come on," Sears bellows. "We *know* you're in there. Where else could you be—right?"

Ha-ha, the joke's on you, Sears! I'm not in my apartment. I'm crouching down next to a corpse and feeling the peculiar sensation of my entire world caving in on me.

I very much need to get out of this apartment with the corpse of the stranger who kind of resembles my almost-boyfriend.

But clearly, I can't return to my apartment, either.

And that's when the panic attack that I've been able to keep at bay these past few minutes comes roaring back. An invisible hand of steel seizes my throat, determined to squeeze the life right out of me. My heart flutters, and it feels like there are bird wings flapping wildly against my rib cage.

Logically, I know it's the classic fight or flight response—a physiological response to a grave threat. And I also know that trying to "fight" or even reason with Sears and Yates would be futile.

Which leaves only one option.

The unthinkable one.

CHAPTER 34

I'M TREMBLING VIOLENTLY as I peek outside the front hallway windows in the third floor stairwell.

I'm half-expecting to see an entire SWAT team assembled, along with a battalion of Secret Service guys, each one of them ready to take me down.

But the corner of 20th and Green is more or less deserted. There are sirens in the distance, most coming from the Parkway. The sun has already slipped behind the buildings of University City, casting the whole block in a sinister shade of darkness.

Downstairs, Yates calls out, and this time his voice is almost pleading with me. "Come on, Tricia. You don't want us busting down your door. Your landlord's gonna make you pay for it."

"Enough of this," Sears says. "Open up this door now!"

But I'd be okay with them destroying my property. Because if Yates and Sears are busy trying to break down my door, I might be able to sneak down the stairs, through the hallway and out the front door before they realize I'm not home.

Did you just hear yourself, Tricia? You? Go outside?

Shut up.

So you can what—die of sunlight and fear in the fresh air?

Seriously, I don't have time for this. My apartment is tiny. Once they're in, Yates and Sears are going to realize I'm not there in about 2.3 seconds. If I'm going to make a break for it, I need to start running *now*.

I steal another glance outside, just to make sure nobody's watching, and then I—

Wait.

Somebody *is* watching.

More precisely…a skinny man, leaning against a parked car, eating—with relish—what looks like a candy bar, is staring at my apartment window three floors below. He might as well be seated in a theater, waiting for the main attraction to begin.

I squint in the near darkness to see if I recognize him. And honestly, I don't. He's kind of a plain-looking guy. Middle-aged. Thin, but otherwise perfectly unremarkable.

But you do recognize him, Tricia. Because you called him just a few minutes ago.

No I didn't. I called Jackson!

The real Jackson is lying dead in the apartment down the hall.

Then who's this creepy stranger?

Come on, Tricia. You're smarter than this. You've got all of the pieces of the puzzle. Now put it together.

And that's when I do.

This is him. No matter what this guy looks like, he's the one who's been misdirecting me from the beginning.

The whole dowdy, middle-aged lady thing? That was a disguise.

He wasn't killing out of boredom or because he just stepped off a train from Crazytown. He specifically created the Mrs. Archer persona so that he could blend in with a crowd of political rally-goers and take out the senator with the arrow. Then he must have shed his disguise like a snake, sloughing off a skin to blend right back into the crowd once again.

And that night, when "Mrs. Archer" was pinging pebbles off your front window? That was just another test, wasn't it?

If you remember, I looked out my window and saw Mrs. Archer, giving me the *tsk-tsk* thing with her finger. Which freaked me out.

And then a minute later, I heard the front door open. I thought it was Mrs. Archer, that she had come to kill me. Instead, it was the man I *thought* was my neighbor—a man I thought was Jackson Dolan.

But that man wasn't really my neighbor.

He was the killer, who used some sort of disguise to *look like* my neighbor—a neighbor whom I'd barely seen, and wouldn't recognize except by the broadest details.

Even thinking back on the features of the dead guy in the bathtub, it becomes clear. That wasn't the same man who helped me build *Amelia III* in my apartment last night.

It was someone else.

It was Mrs. Archer, in yet another disguise.

So how did this killer know about my crush on my neighbor? Well, if he was smart enough to track me down through my fallen drone, he's certainly smart enough to check my Facebook page.

I can't believe it.

For the past couple days, I've been making goo-goo eyes at a *professional assassin*.

CHAPTER 35

Target Diary—Day 13 (The Big Day, continued)

I UNWRAP THE second half of my Snickers bar and finish it while the two police officers force open Miss Patricia Celano's apartment door.

I fold up the wrapper neatly and tuck it back in my pocket. That was a very delicious treat. Definitely worth waiting for. I'm eager for my next assignment to get under way so that I'll have another candy bar to look forward to. Vices, after all, must be kept in check.

If the cops are any good, they'll quickly find what they're looking for: a handmade wrist apparatus, complete with spring-loaded arrow. I quickly slipped through Miss Celano's window, and then tucked it away in a kitchen cabinet once I watched her work up the courage to enter apartment 3-D.

They'll also later realize that Patricia's browser history is full of links to sites that provide detailed instructions on how to make such an apparatus. As well as the usual political paranoia/conspiracy theory blogs, message boards, and social media networks.

And the apparatus, of course, will be analyzed in great detail. Eventually, a group of specialists will prove the weapon to be the one that killed the senator. As well as the young man in apartment 3-D.

But right now, the two cops will call it in, of course, and this block will be swarmed by enough government agents to take down a dictator in a small Latin American country.

Which means I don't have much time.

There are only two ways out of that apartment building. One is through the front door, which I am watching carefully. The other is through a back entrance with an alley that leads out to 20th Street, which I also can see. The rest of the block is dense with brownstones, so there is no way out. Even the cockroaches have to scuttle sideways to make their way from building to building.

Where will you go scurrying, Patricia?

CHAPTER 36

NORMALLY, I'D BE proud of my Sherlock Holmes–like powers of deduction. I mean, gimme some credit here. This is a complicated conspiracy, something that has apparently eluded the US Secret Service, and I've solved it. Go, me!

But there's no time to celebrate, because Yates and Sears have just kicked in my front door, and I have to make my move. Like, right now.

Well, you can forget the front entrance and the back door, because either one will put you in plain view of the assassin.

It's a good point.

And that's assuming you could even make it out either of those doors without losing your mind completely.

It's dark out. The sun has set. I'll be fine. Theoretically…

Just like you were fine last year when you got all dolled up and tried to join your friends for dinner?

I can handle it. I just need an escape plan.

Hmmm. How about you pretend you're a drone?

And what—fly away from here? Very funny.

Do it. You need to survive.

CHAPTER 37

Target Diary—Day 13 (The Big Day, continued)

SIRENS ARE APPROACHING. The police officers have made their call, and I'm sure the cavalry is on its way.

So where is Patricia Celano?

It could be that she's curled up in the fetal position next to her dead "boyfriend," just waiting for a lawyer so that she can plead insanity. Or maybe she tucked herself away in a closet, hoping that the bogeymen will somehow leave her alone.

Poor thing.

I thought we'd have the opportunity for one last dance.

The kind of dance where her feet would leave the ground, and the rope would tighten around her neck until the stars come out.

Well, no use lingering. The authorities will no doubt be combing the entire neighborhood, questioning anyone they encounter. Mind you, I never worry about such encounters. I've beaten a dozen lie detectors. But I'd rather not be stopped and questioned directly in front of the main suspect's apartment. Woe to those who crossed paths with Lee Harvey Oswald on that fateful November day!

I move east on Green, planning to clear the six blocks until I reach the Broad Street subway, which will take me north to the edge of the city. From there, I will disappear completely, like I always do.

But a few strides into my escape, a voice echoes off the brownstones.

"Hey! Jerkface!"

I'm elated. It's Patricia, ready to engage.

But where is she?

I spin around, trying to locate the sound of her voice. But she's not behind me on Green, nor is she in the street.

"Ha! I think I've finally figured out your weakness—you never look up!"

There she is. Up on the rooftops above Green Street. My trembling little shut-in patsy, pretending so hard that she's brave.

But she's failing miserably.

However, I now find myself at a disadvantage, because not only has she figured out the plot, but she's also seen my face. My true face.

And that is a loose end I cannot tolerate.

"Want to know something?" she continues.

"What's that?"

"You looked better in a dress."

My arm twitches instinctively, as if I still have my apparatus attached to my wrist. Wouldn't she be surprised to hear a whooshing sound and then look down to see the back end of an arrow protruding from her chest?

But of course the apparatus is now in the hands of the police. I have to rely on other weapons to take her down.

"What's the matter, tough guy? All out of arrows?"

I stare up at Patricia and merely smile, lulling her into a false sense of victory. Her strategy is easy enough to intuit. Just like in all of the bad TV cop shows, she thinks she can "keep me talking."

But she has no idea what is about to happen to her.

CHAPTER 38

HERE'S THE WEIRD thing about…well, me being so *weird* about venturing outside at night.

I realize now that all of my anxieties were focused on the front door of my apartment building. Over time, I'd convinced myself that I could never pass through it. Not even when the sun was tucked away on the other side of the planet, making it perfectly safe for me to step outside. The door was my prison warden. There was no way I could slip past.

But up here on the roof?

With an aerial view of my beloved Spring Garden?

Hell, this is the vantage point I'd grown to *love* over the past few months. The *Amelia* drones were simply my avatars; *I* was the one who was flying.

I climbed out here, once I realized my only choice was to escape via the roof, and suddenly, being out in the world didn't seem all that crazy.

As I climbed the stairs that would take me to the top of the building, I came up with a plan that would give me a shot at proving my innocence.

All I needed was a way to lure the killer to a particular spot.

So, like I had with everything else in my life, I took the very little resources I had and I improvised. I moved along the tops of the neighboring roofs, mirroring the killer's progress down Green Street. Finally, I saw what I needed and decided to catch his attention.

After I called out to him, the killer spun around, like he had no idea where I was. Just like he failed to spot *Amelia* the first time. I get it now. He's so focused on things at the street level that he forgets to look up at the world above his head.

Then he finally spied me. I taunted him a little more, and he moved his arm out, like he wanted to shoot me with an arrow, just like he had shot my drone. Except, he's probably stashed his fancy little wrist crossbow in my apartment for the cops to find.

Oh, you should've seen the look on his bland little face when I goaded him for not having any arrows. He looked like he wanted to throttle me, stomp on my corpse, and then revive me just to throttle me all over again. But he made a good show of it, smiling like he didn't have a care in the world.

And then *BOOM*—he takes off like an Olympic sprinter at the crack of a pistol, headed straight for the building beneath me.

That's right, Archer. Come and get me.

The killer probably thinks he has me trapped. That we're about to start this long cat-and-mouse chase across the rooftops of Spring Garden, as if it were something from the movie *Vertigo*. I'm leaping across chasms and scrambling over gables and I'll probably end up in some dark alley with my neck snapped.

Well, guess again, Archer.

I might be afraid of the world.

But I'm not afraid of heights.

CHAPTER 39

Target Diary—Day 13 (The Big Day, concluded)

THE MOMENT I step onto the roof is the moment I realize she's gone.

Vanished completely.

Did she jump?

I run to the edge of the building and skid to a halt, checking Green Street below for signs of her twisted, dying body. No such luck. Instead, I spy her using a metal drain pipe to climb down the front of this three-story brownstone. Hand over hand, feet pressed against the wall, guiding her way down.

This will not do.

There is no time to come back to the ground the way I came up onto the roof, so I follow her path over to the edge of the building. I use the drainpipe in the same way. The fittings are older than I thought, and they're caked in rust. This is not a path I'd ordinarily choose, but she's forced me into this position.

Patricia reaches the ground safely and sprints across Green. I redouble my efforts to make it down to street level. I cannot allow her to escape.

There's one major difference between myself and Patricia, however: body weight.

And by the time I'm halfway down, the drainage pipe breaks

loose from its moorings. I attempt to leap free, but I'm already falling by the time I'm twisting my body around, aiming for a relatively soft place to land.

My body slams awkwardly onto a small patch of front lawn, missing the spikes of a wrought-iron fence by a matter of inches. Lucky. But upon landing, the air is hammered from my lungs and my vision blurs. The wave of pain washes over me a microsecond later.

A quick and rudimentary self-exam reveals no broken bones, however. Which is good, because I'm going to need them intact when I choke the life out of this meddling woman.

I scan the block. My prey is jogging south on 19th Street in the direction of Logan Circle. Presumably toward those approaching sirens so she can give my full description to the police.

"They won't believe you!" I yell to her, limping slightly as I move down the street. "All the evidence points to you!"

Patricia looks back over her shoulder at me, sticks out her tongue, then faces forward and accelerates.

Did she honestly stick her tongue out?

I push aside the pain and break out into a full run. The city of Philadelphia fades away like the blurring roadside when you're moving eighty miles per hour down an interstate highway. Right now there are only two things in my world: predator and prey.

And the predator is gaining on its prey.

Without warning, she darts right onto Brandywine, which is a narrow and relatively secluded street, heading back in the direction of 20th Street. This is a poor choice on her part. She was doing better before when she was making her way down toward Logan Circle.

"There is no use running," I call out. "I run all night long. You wouldn't believe the stamina I've developed."

"Yeah, well, good for you," she says before quickly turning the corner.

The nerve of her.

I'm really going to enjoy ending her life.

CHAPTER 40

I'M RUNNING SO fast it's barely registered that I'm actually outside, in the fresh air, for the first time in three years.

So this is what freedom feels like.

Though I suppose it's easy to ignore your hypothetical fears when there's a professional assassin hot and heavy on your trail.

My heart is pounding and my temples are throbbing as I pump my arms and legs. I don't know how much longer I can keep this up. The sound of Archer's footfalls are like a boxer's gloves smacking a heavy bag, and I tense up every time I think they're getting closer. While I'm a fairly slender human being, I'm also woefully out of shape. It's kind of hard to do laps when your apartment is the size of a hotel room.

Fortunately, I don't need much in the way of stamina, because I don't have to run all that far.

When I reach the corner of 20th and Hamilton, I come to a full stop. Then I turn around to face my nemesis. Archer is so startled that he comes to an awkward, almost fumbling halt, pinwheeling his arms a bit. I'll admit it; it's nice to see this jerk out of control.

Still, he tries to recover his cool. "I'm surprised you gave up so soon. I thought there would be a little more fight left in you."

I shove my hands into my pockets and struggle to regain my breath.

"I know I can't beat you in a race."

"Very smart of you to realize that."

"But before you do *whatever* it is you're planning on doing to me," I tell him, "I just need to know one thing."

A bemused grin appears on his face. On most guys it would look charming. On this guy, it comes across as creepy.

"And what's that?"

"How you did it."

"Did what?"

"Take out a senator in broad daylight and then vanish into thin air."

He takes a moment to study me. I mean, *really* study me. As if my question boggled his mind. Finally, after a small eternity, he opens his mouth and speaks again. "You're serious," Archer says.

I bug my eyes out a little, as if to say, *Do you think I'm kidding around here?*

"If we had more time together," he says, "I'd be happy to walk you through the whole plan, step by step. I'm proud of my work. And I've done a lot of it in preparation for this mission. But the clock is ticking. Suffice to say that people always see what they want to see. They're not trained to observe the truly unexpected."

"Like the arrow that magically appeared out of your sleeve," I say.

Archer nods.

"But once the senator was hit, how were you not tackled by a dozen Secret Service guys?"

"Witnesses will swear they saw a woman take that shot. In the confusion, I simply ceased being that woman and transformed into just another panicked spectator. It's easier than you think. The basic principles have been around for centuries."

"Amazing."

Archer smiles. "I'm so glad you're impressed."

I laugh. "No, I'm not impressed by your nerdy Renaissance Faire assassination plan. Arrows? Seriously? No, I think it's amazing you just confessed."

Archer moves closer, attempting to box me in. There's an old storefront behind me. If I try to run in either direction, he'll definitely be able to catch me.

"It doesn't matter that I confessed to you," he says quietly. "You're the only one who heard, and in a few seconds, you will be dead."

"But that's the thing. I'm not the only one who heard."

CHAPTER 41

SAY HELLO, *AMELIA I*.

Yep, she's right above our heads, still caught in the ancient rusty sign on that rooftop where she crashed a while ago. With her little camera trained on this exact location. And she's captured *everything*.

While I was still on the rooftop a couple of minutes ago, I opened her app on my cell phone and saw that she had just enough power to pull this off. Then I texted the link to Officer Yates and told him to watch—This will explain everything.

And then, of course, I climbed down the front of a three-story brownstone and ran like hell, all with a trained killer nipping at my heels.

Oh, the look on Archer's face as he glances up and sees *Amelia I,* notices that there's a blinking green light near her camera, and instantly puts it all together.

What's that old saying? You can fool all of the people some of the time, and you can fool some people all of the time, but not all of the people all of the time?

Well, when a drone is watching you when you're trying to fool people, forget about it. You're screwed.

"What did you do?" Archer snarls. *"WHAT DID YOU DO?"*

I'm about to respond with a wisecrack, but I never get the chance. Because Archer immediately lunges for me.

CHAPTER 42

I'VE SUFFERED THROUGH multiple panic attacks this past week. Each time, I've likened the experience to "hands squeezing my throat" or some other metaphor for strangulation.

Well, let me tell you—a panic attack feels nothing like actually being strangled.

There are no "invisible hands." You feel every bony finger—especially the fat thumbs, crushing your windpipe like it's the cardboard tube inside a roll of paper towels.

Archer doesn't need arrows to kill. His hands are more than capable of pulling off this particular job.

The murder of a nosy shut-in.

Oh, I fight back, for what it's worth. I dig my nails down into his flesh, hoping to strike down into the bones of his hands. But the strength fades from my limbs before I can do anything resembling damage, and I'm sure Archer is so furious he doesn't feel a thing.

It really sucks that the last thing I'm ever going to see is Archer's red, trembling, angry face.

What happens when you die, you might ask? *Do you see stars or clouds? A long tunnel with a bright light at the end? Or simply black nothingness?*

In my case, it's none of the above. Instead, I see faces. Not the faces of long-deceased relatives come to take me home. Still, they are faces I recognize, even though I can't assign names to them.

Why do you all look so familiar? is my last thought before all of the lights turn out.

Later, I would understand why I knew those faces.

CHAPTER 43

THOSE FACES BELONGED to my neighbors in Spring Garden, the very same people I used to watch as they headed off to work in the morning, and then trudged home later that evening, tired or defeated. Some were the people who came home happy, looking forward to spending the night with someone they cared about. I saw them all through the eye of *Amelia* and experienced their lives vicariously.

Lawyer-types in their fine suits and even more expensive shoes who spent their days in air-conditioned conference rooms. Ordinary Philly dudes in jeans and button-down shirts trying to make it to 6 p.m. as fast as they possibly can…

I heard that about a dozen of them were running up to pull Archer off me. He wriggled like a maniac apparently, but there were just too many of them.

One neighbor, a nurse at Pennsylvania Hospital, worked on reviving me while the others subdued Archer, tackling him to the sidewalk.

You have to understand that in Philly, when we make reference to "subduing" someone, what we really mean is that we beat the holy crap out of them. Later, at the trial, Archer's face was still badly bruised and his jaw wired shut. The doctors said he'll never look the same.

Pity.

After all my neighbors saved me, Yates and Sears made it to the corner of 20th and Hamilton in time to slap the cuffs on Archer and read him his Miranda rights. They pretty much got instant credit for the whole thing.

Archer's real name, by the way, turned out to be...

You know what? I don't want to give that creepy guy any more notoriety than he already has. He can remain anonymous in my story.

Besides, to me he'll always be Mrs. Archer, the (supposedly) professional assassin in a dress who got his butt kicked by a shut-in.

CHAPTER 44

AFTER THE WHOLE story made the news, I became *sort-of* famous. You know what they call it now—"internet famous." The kind of fame that lasts for a couple of minutes, tops, before the world is fascinated by, like, somebody in a Chewbacca mask telling knock-knock jokes or a dog who knows how to pump its paws to heavy metal.

Even Yates and Sears made it onto a few talk shows, even though they didn't do much aside from watch a link I'd texted them and show up to finish the job that my Spring Garden neighbors had started.

"We knew you weren't responsible for the senator," Yates later admitted to me.

"Yeah, we just thought you were nutty," Sears added.

Thanks, fellas.

But my brief hit of fame did bring a lot of my old friends out of the woodwork, and they all insisted on taking me out for a drink. Or five.

Which sounds great to me.

No, I'm not cured. My *solar urticaria* is still a consistent source of annoyance and a constant threat to my health. The only way

I ever see my beloved city while the sun is shining down upon it is through the camera lens of a drone. And I use *Amelia I,* if you must know—the original.

Yates pulled the old girl down from that rusty old sign, knocked on my door shyly, and presented it to me as if it were a lost kitten. I felt like hugging the thing, but thought that might be a little weird.

As it turns out, I ended up giving Yates a hug instead. He's not so bad, once you get past the uniform and the beer belly. I invited him in for some instant coffee. Seemed to be the decent thing to do, even if he busted down my apartment door (and yeah, the landlord charged me for it).

"So what would you do if I were to ask you out?" Yates says to me one night, acting shy once again.

"I'd ask how you'd feel about a threesome."

"I'm sorry," he says, choking on his coffee, "w-what did you just say?"

"You heard me. Amelia's gotta chaperone. The thing is, I don't trust the police."

By now, I *have* made my peace with the outside world.

In fact, tonight I'm meeting a couple of my lovely Spring Garden neighbors at my new favorite joint, which happens to be BYOB. It's open only after sundown. There's an amazing view of nighttime Philadelphia, and yet it's never crowded. Best of all, it's a very short walk from my apartment.

Just four flights up.

Private Johannesburg is closing down, after one last assignment . . .

Read on for an extract

THE CLEAN-UP CREW HAD missed a bloodstain. Joey Montague saw it as soon as he lifted the steel filing cabinet. Now dried to a deep rust color, the blood had seeped through a crack in the floorboards, darkening the wood around it.

It was ingrained now, a permanent reminder of the disasters that the past two weeks had brought. Their last contracts cancelled, a devastating burglary, and finally his business partner's suicide. On Wednesday morning, he'd walked in to find Khosi Khumalo's body slumped on the floor with a fatal bullet wound in his temple. In death, Khosi had looked peaceful, and his service pistol was lying near his right hand.

Then, as now, Joey's first reaction had been an anguished, "Why?"

But that question could never be answered. Khosi hadn't even left a note.

The new tenants could worry about removing the floor stain. Joey was vacating the building. After Khosi's death, he'd been tempted to close up shop for good, abandon his hopes and dreams and go back to the corporate world. But in the end, his fighting spirit prevailed and he'd decided simply to scale down. He would run Private Johannesburg from his home office until he was back on his feet—emotionally and financially. He would carry on trying to make a success of Khosi's legacy, even in these difficult circumstances.

He still remembered the call, seven months ago, that had lured him out of his pressurized office job and catapulted him into a different and riskier world.

"Joey? It's me, Khosi! Listen, bro, I've got a great opportunity here. You know I've been running my own show as a P. I. the past few years? Well, on my last case, I ended up working with an international firm called Private. Long story short, Jack Morgan, the owner, proposed that I open a branch here. Private Johannesburg. Bro, this is going to be huge—the potential is unlimited, but I need help. I need a business partner in this venture. I could use your expertise in financial forensics. You want to come discuss it over a whisky after work?"

He'd signed the deal with Khosi that night and resigned from his corporate job the next day, confident he was making the right decision. Now, he was no longer sure.

A gust of wind rattled the wire-fastened window latch, distracting Joey from his thoughts. He didn't have time to stare at the floor; he needed to get the last of the furniture in the truck because a summer storm was approaching fast. Dark thunderheads were swallowing Johannesburg's skyline. The sight of those high-rise buildings, clad in pale concrete and glimmering glass, had become familiar to him. They were a symbol of hope that one day he could move the business out of this humble suburb where rentals were cheap but crime was escalating, and into the CBD. Now, the storm had turned the skyscrapers to a dull, forbidding gray. The trees in the nearby park swayed wildly in the gale, and litter scudded down the sidewalk.

As the first drops of rain spattered the dusty glass, Joey's cellphone started ringing.

"Montague," he answered, leaning his elbows on the cold steel cabinet.

"Is that Private Johannesburg? It's Isobel Collins speaking. I'm looking to hire a bodyguard urgently." The caller sounded breathless and Joey picked up an American accent.

You're a couple of days too late for that, Ms. Collins, Joey thought sadly, as lightning split the sky. He was going to tell her that Khosi, the firm's only qualified bodyguard, had tragically died, but she spoke again.

"Please, I need your help."

Joey caught sight of his own reflection in the darkening glass. Short-cropped black hair, deep-set hazel eyes, hard jaw. His expression was grim, making him look older than his age of thirty-five. Khosi had always joked that Joey lost ten years every time he smiled.

He moved away from the window, where rain was drumming the panes.

"There's nobody who can help," he explained in heavy tones.

"It's urgent." Had she heard him? Perhaps the storm was affecting the signal; her voice crackled down the line.

"What's the problem?" he asked.

"I've just arrived in Johannesburg from JFK. I need a bodyguard for the weekend. I booked someone before I left, but he didn't meet me at the airport."

"I'm sorry. No guards are available." As he spoke, thunder crashed overhead.

"What was that? I didn't hear you. This connection is terrible."

"I said we don't have a qualified guard at this time." He shouted the words, but they were obliterated by the clatter of hail on the roof.

Clearly, the elements were conspiring against him.

"You're on the top of my list," Isobel replied. "Private, I mean. I have other options, but you're my first choice. So if you could . . . I'd really appreciate it."

Joey was about to repeat his refusal, but he hesitated. There was something in her voice that was making him uneasy.

"Please, I'm short of time," she added, and Joey heard a tone in her voice he recognized all too well.

Isobel Collins was badly scared.

Perhaps she was frightened of traveling alone in a country with such a high crime rate. Most visitors were paranoid about safety in South Africa, even though there were always the few who tried to climb out of their safari vehicles to hand-feed the lions.

Suddenly Joey thought: why shouldn't he take the job himself? Although he didn't have practical experience in the field, he'd completed a close-protection course and a self-defense seminar during his first month with Private. Shepherding a tourist around the city would be an easy job, and it would fill the empty weekend ahead that he'd been dreading.

"I'll do it," he promised.

"Thank you," Isobel replied, in a voice filled with relief. "I really appreciate it—it's my first time here, and I feel out of my depth. The city's different than I thought it would be . . . Way bigger, for one thing. And busier."

"Are you still at the airport?"

"No, I've left already. I'm driving to my lodgings."

"Give me the address and I'll meet you there." He assumed she'd be heading to the CBD, where most tourists stayed—although travelers usually came for business, rather than leisure.

Founded in the 1880s as a gold-rush city, Johannesburg had always attracted people looking to make fast money. Today the thriving CBD, in the suburb of Sandton, was filled with an aggressive, contagious energy. Beyond it, in every direction, the city grew and sprawled.

Although Joey found Johannesburg's history and culture fascinating, he had to acknowledge that for the majority of tourists, the place was merely a stop-off point for the more scenic towns and game reserves nearby. But even so, it was where the wealthy people of South Africa lived. It was the country's business hub; where the money flowed and deals were done.

The Sandton CBD was accessible by high-speed train from the airport, and he wished he'd had a chance to tell Isobel, because it was far easier to take the train than fight through Johannesburg's notoriously congested roads.

But, as it happened, Joey had guessed her destination completely wrong.

"I'm staying in Kya Langa," she said.

"You're staying *where*?" He hadn't misheard, but he was hoping she'd gotten the place name wrong.

"Number three Foundry Road, Kya Langa. It's in eastern Johannesburg."

"Yes, I know where it is, I used to do work in the area, but . . ."

Adrenaline flooded through him. Ms. Collins was on her way to one of the most dangerous places in the city, where slum housing had sprung up around an abandoned metal-works factory, causing the lower-income neighborhood to decline drastically. That was just one of the reasons why crime in that part of Johannesburg had spiraled out of control. There were others, even more serious.

Why was she heading there? He wished he knew, but he supposed that as a bodyguard, it wasn't his place to ask. In any case, questions would only waste valuable time.

"I'll get to you as fast as I can," he promised.

ALSO BY JAMES PATTERSON

ALEX CROSS NOVELS

Along Came a Spider
Kiss the Girls
Jack and Jill
Cat and Mouse
Pop Goes the Weasel
Roses are Red
Violets are Blue
Four Blind Mice
The Big Bad Wolf
London Bridges
Mary, Mary
Cross
Double Cross
Cross Country
Alex Cross's Trial (*with Richard DiLallo*)
I, Alex Cross
Cross Fire
Kill Alex Cross
Merry Christmas, Alex Cross
Alex Cross, Run
Cross My Heart
Hope to Die
Cross Justice
Cross the Line

THE WOMEN'S MURDER CLUB SERIES

1st to Die
2nd Chance (*with Andrew Gross*)
3rd Degree (*with Andrew Gross*)
4th of July (*with Maxine Paetro*)
The 5th Horseman (*with Maxine Paetro*)
The 6th Target (*with Maxine Paetro*)
7th Heaven (*with Maxine Paetro*)
8th Confession (*with Maxine Paetro*)
9th Judgement (*with Maxine Paetro*)
10th Anniversary (*with Maxine Paetro*)
11th Hour (*with Maxine Paetro*)
12th of Never (*with Maxine Paetro*)
Unlucky 13 (*with Maxine Paetro*)
14th Deadly Sin (*with Maxine Paetro*)
15th Affair (*with Maxine Paetro*)

DETECTIVE MICHAEL BENNETT SERIES

Step on a Crack (*with Michael Ledwidge*)
Run for Your Life (*with Michael Ledwidge*)
Worst Case (*with Michael Ledwidge*)
Tick Tock (*with Michael Ledwidge*)
I, Michael Bennett (*with Michael Ledwidge*)
Gone (*with Michael Ledwidge*)
Burn (*with Michael Ledwidge*)
Alert (*with Michael Ledwidge*)
Bullseye (*with Michael Ledwidge*)

PRIVATE NOVELS

Private (*with Maxine Paetro*)
Private London (*with Mark Pearson*)
Private Games (*with Mark Sullivan*)
Private: No. 1 Suspect (*with Maxine Paetro*)
Private Berlin (*with Mark Sullivan*)
Private Down Under (*with Michael White*)

Private L.A. (*with Mark Sullivan*)
Private India (*with Ashwin Sanghi*)
Private Vegas (*with Maxine Paetro*)
Private Sydney (*with Kathryn Fox*)
Private Paris (*with Mark Sullivan*)
The Games (*with Mark Sullivan*)
Private Delhi (*with Ashwin Sanghi*)

NYPD RED SERIES

NYPD Red (*with Marshall Karp*)
NYPD Red 2 (*with Marshall Karp*)
NYPD Red 3 (*with Marshall Karp*)
NYPD Red 4 (*with Marshall Karp*)

STAND-ALONE THRILLERS

Sail (*with Howard Roughan*)
Swimsuit (*with Maxine Paetro*)
Don't Blink (*with Howard Roughan*)
Postcard Killers (*with Liza Marklund*)
Toys (*with Neil McMahon*)
Now You See Her (*with Michael Ledwidge*)
Kill Me If You Can (*with Marshall Karp*)
Guilty Wives (*with David Ellis*)
Zoo (*with Michael Ledwidge*)
Second Honeymoon (*with Howard Roughan*)
Mistress (*with David Ellis*)
Invisible (*with David Ellis*)
The Thomas Berryman Number
Truth or Die (*with Howard Roughan*)
Murder House (*with David Ellis*)
Never Never (*with Candice Fox*)
Woman of God (*with Maxine Paetro*)

BOOKSHOTS

Black & Blue (*with Candice Fox*)
Cross Kill
Private Royals (*with Rees Jones*)
The Trial (*with Maxine Paetro*)
Chase (*with Michael Ledwidge*)
113 Minutes (*with Max DiLallo*)
The Verdict (*with Robert Gold*)
French Kiss (*with Richard DiLallo*)
Taking the Titanic (*with Scott Slaven*)
Killer Chef (*with Jeffrey J. Keyes*)
The Christmas Mystery (*with Richard DiLallo*)
Kidnapped (*with Robert Gold*)
Come and Get Us (*with Shan Serafin*)
Hidden (*with James O. Born*)
The House Husband (*with Duane Swierczynski*)
Malicious (*with James O. Born*)
French Twist (*with Richard DiLallo*)